Praise for *The Vixen Amber Halloway*

"LaHines's fascinating narrator, Ophelia, is decidedly patholog-
ical. And here's the surprise—she's also sympathetic, humor-
ous, intelligent—a deeply damaged woman telling her tale to a
prison psychiatrist in preparation for a hearing before a parole
board, but it's not a confession.... The novel raises questions
about diagnoses of mental disorders, possible treatment, and
the appropriateness of incarceration."

—NPR Podcast, *Damn on Books*

"A heart-wrenching account of one soon-to-be ex-wife's psychological breakdown...a compulsive read."

—Katrīna Biele, *Long. Sweet. Valuable*, Medium.com

"*The Vixen Amber Halloway* is dark and compulsive reading.
Following a woman's descent into madness after her husband
leaves her for another woman, this compact and complex novel
pulls you into the mind and delusions of a woman as she slowly
devolves while you watch, helpless to stop it."

—Mary Webber O'Malley, bookseller at Skylark Bookshop

"Carol LaHines has invented here a compulsively readable and
craftily constructed tale of murder and mayhem. Her wonder-
fully original unreliable narrator tells a story that will make you
laugh and cry and perhaps remember Humbert Humbert in
Lolita."

—Sheila Kohler, author of award-winning novels including
Cracks and *Open Secret*

"Carol LaHines excels in a wry blend of humor and darkness... breathtaking in its descriptive psychological draw and surprising in some of its twists and turns of plot. LaHines creates a vivid story of a woman who embarks on a campaign that leads her further into darkness, taking readers by the hand in a dangerous invitation to join in the journey."

—D. Donovan, Senior Reviewer, *Midwest Book Review*

"With pinpoint accuracy, LaHines nabs the inner life of a raging, jerky-eating narrator traumatized by family history who recounts her Lolita-like obsession with allegro turns of brilliance. Ophelia's selective memory, steady wit, and allusions to Dante slip off her tongue with delicious, underhanded humor. Ophelia will make you feel the chill of vengeance, because her fury—delivered in a voice perfectly crafted by LaHines—makes perfect sense."

—Maureen Pilkington, author of *This Side of Water: Stories*

THE VIXEN AMBER HALLOWAY

Carol LaHines

Regal House Publishing

Published by
Regal House Publishing, LLC
Raleigh, NC 27605
All rights reserved

ISBN -13 (paperback): 9781646034666
ISBN -13 (epub): 9781646034673
Library of Congress Control Number: 2023942953

Regal House Publishing, LLC
https://regalhousepublishing.com

Printed in the United States of America

For Lizz and Shannon

1

Some have questioned my sanity. Only a mentally imbalanced woman, they say, would spy on her estranged husband and his lover from a tree. Only a delusional woman would believe that the husband would one day return, when the evidence—viz., engagement to his lover, before the ink on the divorce papers was even dry—was demonstrably to the contrary. Only a woman unconcerned with how she is perceived by the outside world, by former spouses and law enforcement circles alike, would commit her observations of the husband and his lover to eight consecutively numbered spiral-bound notebooks, producing, in three months' time, a comprehensive, incriminating document that would serve to confirm the prosecution's theory that she was a spurned wife with rancor in her heart.

Leona Valentine, of the *Saratoga County Gazette* (investigative reporter of the year, five years running), called the notebooks "the work of a fragile yet malevolent mind." Ms. Valentine cited instances of electronic interference and surveillance of the subjects to show alleged *mens rea*; she retraced the accused's path, admittedly circuitous, to the Home Depot in Schenectady, where the accused purchased certain household items (zip ties, duct tape) she would later use in furtherance of her deranged aims. Jean-Claude, whom the reporter tracked down to a truck stop just north of the US-Canada border, informed Ms. Valentine that I appeared *off* when he encountered me on the night of August 5, 2011, that I was behaving in a furtive manner suggestive of criminal enterprise.

Our actions may all be explained by reference to certain formative experiences: whether we are loved; whether we are well-cared for; whether our parents wish we'd never been born.

There are coruscating wounds, wounds that do not heal. They fester and suppurate.

And so, I remember the last time I saw my mother. The peanut butter and jelly sandwich she made me, sliced on the diagonal, the crusts removed (I could never abide them). It sat on my plate with a note, *Remember I love you, Ophelia.* There was still a moment in time when she was combing my hair, smoothing the cowlicks, *Remember I love you, Ophelia*, that she might have reconsidered, removed the valise from the trunk, forsaken Bob, none of us the wiser. There was still a moment before the screen door clacked against the doorjamb, before she stepped out into the autumnal Saturday, the leaves fluttering to the ground, there to rot and turn to mulch, that she might have thought the better of her plan to escape to Florida with the used car salesman.

But she stepped over the threshold, *clack*, never looking back.

The prison psychiatrist counsels me to reimagine the past. To return to the pivotal moment, to imagine the dialogue as it should have taken place. *I'm so sorry but I have to leave, I am in love with another man, your father just wouldn't understand.* She has me play the part of my mother, to enable me to see events through her eyes. She has me switch, play the part of my eight-year-old abandoned self, to impress upon me the fact that it wasn't my fault. She gives me a supportive foam pillow and encourages me to take out my aggression against the mother who left, the mother frozen in time. She tells my adult self, the supposedly rational and reasonable self, to embrace the eight-year-old girl, to protect her, to scold the adults who were supposed to protect her but instead failed miserably.

Say what you want to say to her, she prods me. *She never gave you the opportunity. She left you alone. To fend for yourself. Say what you want to say to her now.*

What is there to say? I can pummel the therapeutic pillow, I can rip out its stuffing, but to what end? Nothing can alter the past. No amount of therapeutic role-playing or imaginative gestalt can change the script. The groove in my psyche is too deep.

Why did you leave me? Say it.

I cross my arms, stop role-playing.

Why did you leave me? Say the words.

I examine the diplomas on the wall. I play with the desk toy. One ball knocks into the next, initiates a chain reaction. Ticktock. Set a ball in motion and certain immutable laws come into play, laws of gravity and momentum, laws of fate and inevitable consequence.

2

I rehearse my speech for the parole board. I review my life as dispassionately as possible under the circumstances. I try to understand, but not to excuse. My attorney advises me to accept blame for my actions and to express remorse, and if possible, to apologize directly to Amber's surviving kin. Only by acknowledging and accepting full responsibility for my actions will I achieve absolution. If I fail to accept responsibility, if I maintain my innocence or otherwise protest, I will be sent back to the cell from whence I came.

I will do my best to appear contrite. I will hang my head. I will allude to the crime only in the most general terms so as not to inflame the passions of the spectators. I hope they will be moved to pity by my woeful appearance. I have not spent the last ten years pumping iron or working on my core. I do not spend time in the gym, furiously skipping rope, but have let myself go. I wear dated aviator spectacles—the State of New York, alas, does not carry the same stylish frames as Lens Crafters.

I must sit quietly, listening respectfully, as Amber's friends and relatives line up to read their victim impact statements. How Amber loved to skip rope as a child, how very much she enjoyed Bavarian cream pie. I imagine what they might say:

You took her from me! I will never see my daughter again. I can only visit her grave, and send a prayer heavenward, hoping it will reach her.

My sister is gone. She was more than a sister. She was my best friend, my confidante. And now she can't come to my wedding. She'll never see her nieces and nephews. She's just a name chiseled on a headstone.

My daughter was the light of my life. Why did you have to take her from me?

I will hang my head and listen. I will be wearing prison-issue garb, a heavily laundered jumpsuit that does not flatter.

I will resist making excuses. I will not refer to my wastrel childhood, to the adults who failed to shelter and to care for me. I will not seize upon clear evidence of dysfunction, a family history of mood regulation disorders. Exhibit A, the abandonment by Mother. I will stress my commitment toward rehabilitation, my eagerness to serve the community, citing my work with prison illiterates and others less fortunate than I.

3

Spring 2005

I was a college professor, a scholar of Dante and the harrowing oeuvre. Other than the occasional faculty soirée, I did not socialize much. I preferred to sit at home in my moldering Victorian with my books and research materials on the Hellmouth, a contraption popular in medieval morality plays.

An acquaintance proposed to fix me up. I was in my thirties and not getting any younger, etc. Larissa's husband had a colleague at Halford Medical Supply who was *to die for*. Andy Fairweather, director of sales, northeast region. You sold laparoscopes, guidewires, surgical robots, devices that allowed surgeons to visualize the innards with little-to-no-trauma, a veritable medical miracle.

I hesitated. I'd had but one prior relationship of note, and that had ended badly when he accused me of being cold, detached. Emotional expression is, for the heavily traumatized, a dangerous proposition.

Larissa prevailed upon me to give it a try. What did I have to lose? How many nights could I spend alone watching *Hoarders* and writing papers for obscure academic journals like *The Psychopomp*?

I made a reservation at Milford's on the Lake. I arrived first and was seated at a table by the window. The lake was stocked with pairs of mating swans, gliding by as their feet paddled furiously below the water line. I gnawed on items in the breadbasket, an anxious habit of mine.

"Would the mademoiselle like another roll?" asked the waiter.

"No, thank you." I blushed. He used a file to brush away the crumbs.

You arrived late, apologizing profusely. "Third-quarter sales push!" you lamented. "Never mind. I don't want to bore you."

"It's all right." I listened as you explained the benefits of the Penetrate-R, a breakthrough in noninvasive surgical technique. You were, as advertised, handsome. Your eyes an impossible-to-define shade of blue or green, their color depending on the light.

"Larissa says you're a professor."

"Yes." Medieval literature was filled with harrowers and heretics and Florentine politicos consigned, unfairly or not, to eternal damnation.

"You know, you're very attractive," you said.

I blushed. I'd never been the object of much male attention. I was too cerebral; I didn't make an effort; I was content to hide in formless clothing, etc.

You stared at me. A gaze so penetrating I could not look away. There was a spot of blood on your cheek where you had nicked yourself with the razor.

I invited you in. Soon, we were throwing off our clothes, searching for illumination, tripping over the steps in our haste to make it to the bedroom. "You are so beautiful," you murmured, fumbling with my buttons and fasteners. "I don't think I can hold back." You lifted me off the floor and carried me up the stairs.

"I want to please you," you said, caressing my breasts, kissing me, a breadcrumb trail to the throbbing source of my every aching desire. When I could bear it no longer, when I was babbling sacrilege, my legs trembling uncontrollably, pleading, *Right there, don't stop, don't stop, please don't stop,* you entered me and brought us to an ecstatic communion.

It all seems improbable now, with the missives going back and forth between our respective lawyers, your star-turn testifying for the prosecution, the damnable he-said, she-said of our inevitably disparate accounts. *I tell you, she burned with hate for Amber. She blamed her for everything. No way was this an accident.*

Perhaps one day you will be able to put aside the rancor in your heart and at last see things from my perspective.

4

SUMMER 2005

We made love for hours, long, drawn-out decrescendos of pleasure. You liked to run your fingers over the surgical site, watching, over time, as even the shallow depressions filled in, turned shimmery white, and disappeared.

I'd never had a lover who was so attentive. Who knew, intimately, the ridge of my ear, the incurve of my belly, the slight dent I have in my skull (the result, apparently, of vigorous use of forceps during delivery). Who knew I favored right side over left, as evident from uneven development of the quadriceps and gluteals; who knew I ground my teeth at night, accounting for jaw fatigue and ice-pick headaches. Who knew from the outline of a scar, only barely perceptible, that I'd once undergone emergency surgery for a ruptured appendix, an undiagnosed condition my father, drunk on Jack Daniels, had failed to appreciate, even after I'd fallen over, clutching my side, complaining of tell-tale pain in the lower right quadrant. *Stop being dramatic*, he'd said.

You had an interruption in your clavicle, where once you had fallen from a jungle gym. A slight deviation in your septum. A keloid scar on your shin, the result of a fall off a bicycle. You'd broken your nose, and suffered a collapsed lung, but prompt medical attention, together with your parents' insistence that a plastic surgeon close the wound, had minimized the damage, speeded up the healing process, made you almost good as new. *Almost good as new*, you liked to say. You'd escaped, virtually unscathed, from life.

We slept tangled in one another, bodily rhythms synchronized. The ba-BUMP of our hearts, the gurglings of our internal organs. We search for the one who completes us, the one who will make us whole. That person was you.

5

We married in the fall season. You, me, the justice of the peace of Saratoga County. I had no father to walk me down the aisle; my mother, the one who abandoned me at the tender age of eight, leaving me effectively on my own, was living in Pensacola, miles away, persona non grata.

Your parents worried whether we were perhaps rushing into things, committing too hastily to lifelong union. They prevailed upon us to *give it some time*. They gave us a leaded crystal punch bowl.

We had a hastily organized reception at Milford's on the Lake. Two tables, pushed together to accommodate our guests. We waltzed to "You Light Up My Life" and fed each other angel food cake with buttercream icing.

You said you were so very lucky to have met me. Our love was an impossible-to-explain gift. You serenaded me. You sang about lighting up my life and filling my nights with song. The words echo across the years. Our guests clapped and toasted us, *to a long and happy life.*

A long and happy life.

6

We honeymooned at Mohonk, an old mountain house on the shores of a glacial lake. We slept on a brass bed, entwined in one another. In the morning, after a hearty breakfast of the all-you-can-eat variety—omelets, french toast, crisp bacon—we set off for a hike. We took the Skytop trail to a viewing point overlooking the Rondout Valley. The sky was cloudless and unwritten upon, our voices echoing off the rock face, *We are here, we are here.*

We rounded the lake, arriving at a sign for the Labyrinth with a jagged arrow indicating the ascent. Perhaps we might have reflected on the advisability of embarking on a hike up the rock face clad in little more than tennis shoes and swimsuits. Perhaps we should have read the warning on the handy foldout map the clerk had given us, indicating *falling rocks* and other debris and warning away those with cardiac or other conditions that might prove fatal. Instead, we entered blithely. We scrambled over the rock, squeezed ourselves between granite slabs, becoming stuck in the narrower passages.

"This is, uh, harder than I thought," I said. I could not help but rue the heavy breakfast.

You were remarkably calm, untroubled (you always were). You pulled me through the narrow spots, yanked me upward, dragged me over granite slabs. If you were under strain, you gave no tell. A lifetime of weightlifting and cardio fitness had made of you a finely muscled and capable rescuer.

"It'll be okay," you promised, kissing my forehead. "There's nothing to be afraid of." You laughed. You gamboled across the rock face, leapt over crags, avoiding treacherous obstacles like a hundred-foot vertical drop (the Devil's Larder, according to the map). You were always so deft at eluding trouble, be it dodging a meddlesome colleague or figuring out the best way to scale a glacial erratic. Nothing rattled you; nothing gave you pause; nothing caused you to awaken, screaming, in the middle of the night. It was one of the qualities I most admired in you—your self-assuredness in sharp contrast to my own negligible self-worth and fragile self-image, the echo of Mother's leave-taking.

"We're almost there. I can see the end of the trail. Come on, you can do it. I believe in you." You were a bronze idol, glistening in the sun.

At last, exhilarated and delirious, we reached the summit. I gazed into the pit of the valley, the mountain house in the distance. All around us, the murmuring evergreens, their bladed whispers. The scent of pine heavy in the air. You took me in your arms and kissed me.

"We are here," you cried, your words reverberating off the granite rockface, filling the valley.

"We are here," I said, overlapping echoes.

For the rest of our stay, we would stick to the carriage routes, the herb garden, the less strenuous walking trails, avoiding the switchbacks and anything marked as *difficult ascent* on the trail map.

7

You drew me out. You encouraged me to express what I felt inside. You comforted me during seemingly interminable blue spells and crying jags, helping me to recast the past as a character-building exercise instead of a soul-coring enterprise. I was no less worthy because Mother had left, choosing the used Cadillac salesman over me.

You taught me to love myself and to take pride in my achievements. *It's no small thing*, you said, to have a doctorate in medieval literature, to have defended myself against a board of academics intent on demolishing my thesis regarding just punishments. *No small thing* to have authored a monograph on the role of the psychopomp—a guide to the underworld, typically a blind sage or a decrepit philosopher—in the harrowing oeuvre.

We took breakfast together in the mornings. You, an energy drink; me, a bagel with a generous smear of cream cheese. I read the *New York Times*; you, the sports page of the *Saratoga County Gazette*. The early morning light flooded the kitchen nook, bathing us in its glow.

In the evenings, we sat on the couch, watching marathons of *Hoarders* and *My 600-Pound Life*, tittering as Glenda made life-and-death decisions between disposing of the souvenir trays or the umpteenth plastic lid. Ella was living in her car after her husband left her, displaced by the weight of her possessions, the square footage of the house given over to mountains of out-of-season clothing. *Yes or no?* the hoarding specialist demanded, presenting a stark choice between a troll and Smurfette—a *double bind*, in the parlance, that gave the hoarder the illusion that he or she had a choice in the matter.

We slept together on the old featherbed, limbs entwined, pulses synchronized. My head in your armpit, your torso in the small of my back, my hair draped over your forearm.

The splitting of the bamboo was our favorite position: left leg pinned under the man's right, right leg flung over his left shoulder, allowing for the deepest penetration. You scraped my insides, inflamed my *van Grafenberg* nerve locus, filling my empty spaces.

"Deeper," I groaned, dissolving in ecstasy.

8

I wanted to sell the old Victorian and buy a new home, but you convinced me it would be foolish. The house had character. It was a rare example of the Queen Anne style, with flourishes like gables and overhanging eaves. It had good bones, whatever else may have transpired on the premises during my turbulent childhood.

We set about restoring the house. We watched *This Old House* and *Fixer Upper*, shows that taught us how to make a dental ledge or rewire old fixtures or make a table from reclaimed wood. We stripped layers of accumulated grime to discover hammered tin ceilings. We re-stained the oak floors and the neglected wood furnishings that had been left to fester in the damp of the basement. We restored the grandeur of the central staircase—curved walnut banister and ornate newels in the style of the era.

After prodding, you convinced me to throw out the junk in the attic. Boxes of my father's old patent applications. Family photos that had been damaged by water infiltration, their edges damaged by mold.

"What are you holding on to?" you asked.

We were proud of what we had built together, proud of our handiwork and ingenuity and facility with a lathe and a circular saw. A self-contained, hermetic world. You, me, our Craftsman tools.

In the evenings, we sat on the porch, the night deepening, the chirrup of cicadas that had emerged from their lairs after seventeen years' confinement.

9

Iwas not enthusiastic about having children—what did I know about raising another human being, about love and sacrifice, saying *there, there* and wiping snot and explosive bowel movements? After age eight, when Mother left, I was more or less on my own, left to forage for nourishment and to avoid upsetting my father.

You would make a great mom, you told me. According to you, I was not ill-suited to motherhood; I was merely missing examples.

You wanted to have three, maybe four children. You were going to build a treehouse in the hundred-year-old elm in the backyard. It could withstand the weight, you assured me, despite three bouts with Dutch elm disease.

When I failed to conceive after a year or two, you told me not to despair. The medical literature was filled with examples of women who'd conceived years after giving up, who had surprise babies in their forties, who adopted only to get pregnant with twins. It was only a matter of time.

A matter of time.

10

September 2010

We celebrated our fifth wedding anniversary, defying naysayers and skeptics who thought our union to be hasty and ill-thought-out. Even your parents were forced to admit that they had been wrong, retracting criticism that I was too old for you, too *glass half-empty*.

We returned to Lake Mohonk. The head waiter served up an angel food cake with buttercream icing and topped with five sparklers, one for each year of wedded bliss. The resident lounge singer regaled us with a swing version of "You Light Up My Life."

We renewed our vows in the tulip garden. The Unitarian pastor asked whether we intended each to take the other, in sickness and in health, in good times and bad; whether we swore to love one another to death do us part, mutatis mutandis. What God has joined together let no man tear asunder, etc. The birds swooped down, as if on cue, falling and rising in effortless murmuration. A butterfly fluttered by and landed on my bouquet. A blue-tailed swallow, according to Pastor Joe, who happened to be an amateur lepidopterist. The butterfly was shimmering, iridescent; it rubbed its feelers together in the way insects do, as if they are plotting or worrying over something.

The pastor remarked that he'd seldom seen a happier couple. *What was our secret?* he asked, slapping you on the back and upsetting your balance. He was a large man with little awareness of his physical strength.

We walked along the carriage route to the top of the mountain. Looking down, we shouted, *We are here*, our voices amplified by the acoustical pit of the rock face, granite outcroppings

hundreds of millions of years old, the terminus of the Lauren-
tide ice sheet. Over centuries, the valley had been worn down
by the elements, shaped by wind and corrosive forces.

"I have something for you," you said. An eternity band, a
perfect circle representing our union.

"Oh, Andy! How did you smuggle this in?"

"I have my ways." You winked. "I love you."

We made love in the glen, the birds tittering above and the
sun beating down on us. The world so very bright, the sky a
heartbreaking blue. You, me, our bodies melded together (not in
the least because we were sweating and some burrs had affixed
themselves to our tender parts). It was not quite the *splitting of
the bamboo,* but it was at the very least *suspended congress.* If I blink,
I can still see the afterimage. The sentinel pines, the clearing,
the chafing grass. It is burned into my psyche, indelible, like the
moment before Mother left, the piercing blue sky, the clack of
the screen door, before the world shifted irreparably, thrown
off its axis.

11

FALL/WINTER 2010

Happy times tend to run together. Time frolicking naked in the meadow, devouring freshly picked strawberries. Time lying together on the old featherbed, envisioning our future, the children we would eventually have. Shared evenings in the den, reading side-by-side (you, the technical specifications for the Halford surgical dummy; I, Dante's account of the harrowing of Hell), stopping every so often for a peck or a cuddle.

Happiness has an indefinite aspect. Unhappiness, however, is obdurate. It takes hold of the memory. It eludes forgetfulness.

The hang-ups began in the fall. Only when you were home, never when you were away, as if the caller knew your schedule. I found you crouched in low spaces, hidden in the rhododendron bush, *caller interruptus.* If I'd been a woman who placed stock in popular magazines, with their sexual do's and don'ts, their advice for making oneself appealing to a man (Appear confident! Brazen! Take the sexual initiative!, etc., etc.), multiple choice quizzes for estimating the likelihood that your man is cheating on you, breaking your heart, I might have been more perceptive:

Does he take the garbage out and fail to reappear for an hour or more?

Does he hide the telephone bills? Is he always exceeding his minutes?

Does he spend an excessive amount of time primping, smoothing his hair, gazing at his reflection in the mirror, marveling at how handsome he is?

Does he have new techniques in his sexual repertoire? Is there a subtle but detectable difference in the way he caresses you or brings you to climax?

I knew that something was amiss. Having a mother who left me out of the blue, no word of forewarning, not even a *goodbye, have a nice life*, has made of me an exquisite sign reader, seeing imminent disaster, *leave-taking, abandonment*, where there is only mild irritation.

One evening, midway through cleaning out the gutters, you stomped back into the house and flung open your laptop, needing the contact information for a crucial client. You clicked on your email, entering your password—which I could not help but divine by following your keystrokes—L-A-P-A-R-O-T-O M-Y.

Of course! So deviously simple. I committed the password to memory, repeating it under my breath.

The note, once sounded, cannot be unstruck.

Later that night, as you snored contentedly, I snuck back downstairs. I opened your laptop, clicked on your email, entered the password, typing with trepidation, and voilà—found myself scrolling through the mail in your inbox. It was filled with clutter, spam, emails you had inexplicably failed to expunge, everything from *Viagra, cheap!*, to innumerable invitations to join LinkedIn. Your life was never orderly.

I clicked on several promising emails but was dismayed to find only professional correspondence of the most tedious sort—stale jokes, email chains, uploaded photos of an overweight officemate bending over the photocopier. I had just about given up, chastising myself for my lack of faith in you, for my vivid imaginings of what you might be doing with the invisible object of your affections, when I happened upon an email from a coworker named ahalloway@halfordmcd.com. *Room 245, Holiday Inn Topeka—WOW*, with a horrid, leering emoji. Any doubt as to the meaning of the email was elucidated by subsequent correspondence, e.g., *Your ass is fly*. And: *Want to die in your body.* And: *Wife teaching tues and thurs afternoons, u can just come here.*

Imagine my distress! Not only were you embroiled in an affair with a coworker—only the most obvious kind of entanglement—but she was a miserable speller, utterly indifferent to the rules of grammar. She was the kind of person who punctuated sentences with emojis. She expressed herself via majuscule (UR SO HOT). She interpolated exclamation marks after every sentence—sometimes midsentence!—to indicate fetid longing.

And you had invited her into our home—the place we inhabited together, most sacred of spaces—for a romantic afternoon interlude.

I could not erase what I had seen. I resisted the impulse to delete your email accounts and cache of alluring portraiture. What good would it do?

Once confronted, the adulterer will sink further underground, develop more clever passwords, open new email accounts, devise cover names for the love object, something innocuous like Herman or Harry—an opposite-sex beard who will serve as cover-up and diversion for anyone snooping aimlessly through his accounts, looking to initiate divorce proceedings. The adulterer who knows he is under suspicion, whose whereabouts are questioned, whose responses are met with an eye roll and a dismissive *whatever,* will cover his tracks.

I decided to keep silent. And wait.

You were not inclined to think of me as a potential spy, to peg me as a cyber-harasser—indeed, one day, when I had carelessly forgotten to mark one email unread, you simply ascribed it to computer glitch, not even thinking for a moment that I had hacked into your account and was following, via live stream, your chatter with Amber.

I would check your email once in the morning, once in the evening (eventually I lost track). I derived an especial pleasure from interfering with your plans, e.g., *It appears my tire is unexpectedly flat!,* or *My mother is thinking of visiting this weekend!* Like a conductor—violin please, emphasis on the downbeat—I was able to accentuate certain lines, paint orchestral colors.

You and Amber professed your love to one another. You cited me as a nagging interference. You dreamed of eloping (evidently ignorant of bigamy laws). I would not be taken by surprise, as I had been, lo those many years ago, when Mother kissed me on the head, smoothed my hair, *Remember I love you, Ophelia*, before disappearing forever.

I might have left matters alone, meticulously documenting your adulterous activities in the event of divorce proceedings, else waiting for the affair to reach its natural end. Your interest in Amber was in large part attributable to novelty and the thrill of covert assignation. The Amber who skinny dipped in the Marriott Courtyard, or flashed you discreetly on breaks from tedious staff meetings (*your tits are &^*@ incredible!* you crowed), would undergo inevitable transformation in a domestic setting.

But I could not help myself.

Following a steamy weekend at the Marriott Courtyard (you had conference rooms to set up, and cadavers to procure from medical colleges, but you still found time to frolic in the pool, and make love on the black tar rooftop), I could no longer hold back. Pretending to be sexyamber@gmail.com, I electronically severed your relationship. I purported to have found someone else, conveniently at the same convention. A guidewire man from Minneapolis. I was terribly sorry, but, hey, weren't you married, after all? Weren't you breaking vows or transgressing social norms, etc. I interspersed emojis and exclamations, doing my best to simulate Amber's voice. But in the end (Was it the lack of misspellings? My insistence on interpolating [sic], unable to abide unacknowledged errors?), you realized that someone, in all likelihood *me*, had hacked into your email.

"How could you violate my privacy!" you screamed, outraged at the electronic trespass.

"You read my email! You're sending fake messages! That's sick!" you screamed at me, red-faced.

"What's wrong with you?" you continued to harangue me.

"Don't you have anything to say for yourself?" You threw a lamp across the room, shattering same.

"Aren't you going to respond?" you fumed.

You have accused me of a lack of feeling. Of being "out of touch" with my inner self, of being emotionally disconnected, unable to mimic a genuine emotion. Having had parents attentive to every whim, urged to express yourself, every fleeting emotion and impulsive urge, you were accustomed to voicing your feelings, to recognizing them, to articulating them with excruciating precision. *I'm feeling a bit down today after Roger chewed me out at the meeting. I wish I could reel off specifications like Doug, I feel inadequate. Maybe we could go to the lake today, I'm in the mood for fun.* You had no idea what it was like to have to suppress every emotion you'd ever had, to bawl into your fist, to disarm the rifle every night and lock it in the gun cabinet, lest your father make good on his promises and leave you an orphan, utterly alone, as opposed to a motherless child with an abandonment complex and grave doubts as to her own self-worth.

If you expressed an emotion, you were given a cookie or a pat on the back for using your words. I, on the other hand, was slapped across the face, told to shut up, and to get out of my father's sight. I looked like her; I had the same irritating mannerisms (the way I stifled my sneezes; even the way I slept, with one eye open and a leg hanging off the mattress). *So help me you are the spitting image of her,* my father would say, usually when he was slamming a door in my face.

"What were you thinking?" you screamed, shattering a glass, leaving shards everywhere.

I shrugged.

"I'm leaving," you said. You did not say where you were going. I had the relevant contact information in any event. "Call me if any of this has penetrated your skull." The screen door clapped after you. The frame shook, and then you were gone.

NB: You did not apologize. You forgot to add, during the course of your one-sided diatribe, how terribly sorry you were for having broken your marriage vows, for undermining my confidence, for rendering me lonely and insecure and ever more likely to resort to my emergency prescription of Serenifix, PRN, for the relief of debilitating anxiety. You failed to give me the courtesy of even the simplest acknowledgment. *Yes, you were right, I was skulking about, it wasn't all in your head, my moodiness, the distance, the constant rebuffing, it was all motivated by guilt, and fear of capture, please accept my deepest apologies.*

NB: You did not deny the affair. You did not deny what I had uncovered stumbling haplessly through your email (you might have thanked me for moving items into your spam folder!), looking for the truth. You did not deny having arranged to meet Amber at the Marriott Courtyard, on September 20th, for the frolic in the pool. You did not deny meeting her at the Minnie Ha Ha motel, every Tuesday evening, a standing appointment you were loath to cancel, even when I begged you to stay at home, to have a seat next to me on the sofa, we'd both been so busy, wouldn't it be nice to catch up? (*Wife nagging me. Be a little late,* you had emailed, ever so sensitively, just after you had departed.)

You said: *I've done nothing wrong.* A lofty pronouncement for someone caught in flagrante delicto, with his pants down. For someone who sexted and had photos of his naked girlfriend wrapped around a stripper pole.

I eave her out of it, you screamed at me. On the one hand, maintaining your innocence; on the other, *assuming arguendo* the truth of my accusations, begging me to leave her alone, to give her a pass, she was not blameworthy in her own right.

Leave her out of it. As if she were not an integral member of our love triangle, a gravitational force you could not resist. A temptress, a seductress, a tart with a knack for pornographic self-portraiture. I will never be able to erase the images of her tangled in bed sheets, or brushing her teeth topless, or jumping on a trampoline, proving to the world, beyond the shadow of a doubt, that she was not filled with silicone or saline—her breasts the bountiful, genuine article.

How could I leave her out of it? If not for her, we would still be together, sitting on the sofa, watching reruns of *Law and Order*. We would be walking through the woods, listening to the nattering pines. We would be sipping Slurpies, or riding down the post road together, attending faculty receptions together as man and wife, rather than estranged wife, *solo*.

But for Amber, you would still be here. You might be sexting photos of yourself to an unknown someone across cyberspace, but you would still be here. But for Bob, of Bob's Cadillac Emporium (*We will not be undersold!*), my mother would never have left. She would have stayed, caring for me, taking me to school in the Buick Skylark. Whatever mutual enmity she and father might have enjoyed would have dissipated. We might have vacationed in the Poconos or paddled out on Lake George or scaled the glacial erratics of the Shawangunks.

Instead, I have a hole in my heart the size of a shotgun wound.

12

Adultery, from the Latin *adultere, ultere*, on the other side, extra-marital. An offense against God, a violation of the sacred bonds of matrimony, a mortal sin (*Thou shalt not covet thy neighbor's wife, Thou shalt not commit adultery*, the proscriptions could not be clearer), grounds for divorce in all fifty states. It is still technically a criminal offense to sleep with a woman other than your wife, to fornicate with her, to copulate, from the Latin *copulare*, fastened together.

But for your affair with Amber, I would not be sitting in this cell. I would not be ruminating over the course of our relationship, mulling over my remarks to the parole board. I would not be serving concurrent terms of fifteen to twenty-five years, based on aggravating factors like a depraved mind and lack of remorse.

The jailhouse paralegal (serving a life sentence for murder in the second degree, no chance of parole) has advised me to show sympathy toward Amber. To lament the life cut short. To express emotion, if possible, indicating that I am not beyond redemption or rehabilitation or reintegration into society. To sob, but not to overdo it. To sniffle on the sleeve of my orange jumpsuit. *She was a great sales representative, a good friend, a loving daughter, she may have had a thing for married men, but, hey, we all have our faults...*

Contrary to what has been written in the *Saratoga County Gazette* by Leona Valentine, I regret my actions. I wish that I could go back in time, erase the incriminating frames, everything that transpired on the night of August 11, 2011. I wish that I would have learned to better cope with life's stresses, rather than snapping under the weight of so much pent-up aggression. Surely, there were better strategies for coping with life's tribulations—a foam pillow designed to absorb the blows of life's traumas—

rather than terrorizing the real-life strumpet who had broken up my marriage, the homewrecker, the despoiler of my happiness.

Whatever my feelings toward Amber, and however justified, nothing can condone or excuse my actions. Cyber-harassment is a serious crime. Uploading naked photographs to web-sharing sites is no small offense. The emotional distress occasioned by knowing 5,232,001 visitors have slobbered over your breasts is unimaginable.

For all of the above, I am truly sorry.

As for the rest, well, it is difficult to go there. My mind has blotted out many of the details: a self-protective amnesia; a refusal to entertain reality. A well-documented phenomenon in cases of extreme trauma. The prison psychiatrist assures me that the memory is there, somewhere, buried deep in the unconscious. We have only to mount an assault against the psychic defense mechanisms, to slip inside the heavily guarded citadel, and unleash the repressed prisoner. I am liberally medicated with Serenefix, for the relief of anxiety, and Risperate, a mild anti-psychotic. She tells me to relax, to sink deeper into myself, let the world fade away.

You are going deeper, the prison psychiatrist intones. I hear the words as if underwater. I am no longer in the prison medical ward, on the cot that serves as psychiatrist's couch, but deep within, a part of myself that is impenetrable. *You can enter*, she tells me, my Virgil, my psychopomp, as I sink deeper in these unconscious waters. She senses a level of resistance to the psychoanalytic process, psychic debris that must be cleared away before we can continue our journey. An avalanche of ill feelings and traumatic childhood events that must be dealt with.

What do you remember? she asks. (She is supposed to generate a comprehensive psychiatric report by the end of next week. We have a lot of ground to cover, many miles of psychic terrain before a recommendation can be made as to whether I deserve to be paroled.)

I shrug. I cannot proceed further, not now. Even after interrogating myself, enduring cross-examination by Reginald

Wright, Esquire, of the Saratoga County district attorney's office, two days of combative exchanges and testimony that ultimately proved damaging to my case (viz., the admission that I had purchased duct tape and rope at the Home Depot a week prior to the night in question), I am unable to recount the entire story. There are gaps in the narrative, telling lacunae.

13

I returned from the college to find your vehicle in the drive. Any hope of a rapprochement was quickly dashed. A police cruiser was parked behind you. Sheriff Brody, of the Saratoga County police department, introduced himself and served me with a temporary restraining order, prohibiting me from communicating with or even being in the vicinity of the happy couple.

"Sorry, ma'am," the sheriff offered, as I gazed upon the writ. It forbade me from electronically interfering with or in any way appropriating your online identity and email passwords.

You disappeared inside to retrieve some belongings. The sheriff patted me on the back. No doubt trying to gauge whether my threats of being unable to live without you were just words, the result of shock, or whether he needed to summon mental health services. Attempting to determine whether *I don't want to go on* was uttered in exasperation, or an accurate reflection of my precarious mental state.

I assured him that I did not intend to harm myself. I would be all right. At least a reasonable simulacrum of all right. A lifetime of disappointment had left me with certain coping skills.

"It'll be over soon," he assured me.

You tumbled out with a suitcase and a box of medical supplies. You told the sheriff you'd gotten what you needed and were ready to leave. I wanted to scream, to shout out, to whack you over the head, but I was precluded from menacing your person or even addressing you directly. Any form of physical or nonverbal contact was prohibited by the terms of the restraining order, lest I be subject to charges of aggravated harassment, a class E felony, and dispatched to the county jail forthwith. Sheriff Brody advised me to keep a cool head.

I looked away, willfully dissociating myself, trying to erase the foregoing from my mind.

"I'll get the rest of my stuff after things have calmed down," you said. "You're going to be all right, aren't you?" Evincing a sudden concern for my welfare, my tenuous state of mind. Demanding assurances that I would not maim myself, or do something stupid. Imploring me to *get some help*.

"I didn't mean for this to happen. It just did," you offered by way of belated apology.

I shook my head. *Be gone!* I would say, if able to articulate, if able to murmur an intelligible syllable. If able to communicate with you without the threat of imprisonment or aggravated charges.

The screen door clacked behind you, and you were gone.

The heart, ripped from its moorings, soon stops beating.

Left abandoned, alone in the house, a woman will rapidly decline. She will murmur to herself, obsessively reread emails she has copied onto her hard drive, trying to figure out when, exactly, feelings toward the other intensified, when allegiances shifted, when the husband decided to renounce the marriage, to withdraw his affections, as inalterably as if he had uttered, *I divorce thee*, three times in succession.

She will read frank assessment of her character (*wife pain in my ass*). She will learn that her husband, unbeknownst to her, has a fondness for pet names (*sugar plum, hot bod*). She will learn that their tryst was not confined to the soiled bed sheets of the Minnie Ha-Ha motel, but transpired under her nose, in the marital bed, every other Wednesday.

She will learn that she is a pain in the ass, a pathetic lover, emotionally disconnected, impossible to talk to. She is always in a sour mood. She does not appreciate his many kindnesses, the way he makes coffee, or tidies up the sofa pillows.

Though he has an interest in painting himself as an injured party, rather than a devious philanderer, these assessments will nonetheless cause her pain. They will cause her to howl, intermittently, as she goes about her business, tidying up, reorganizing the closet. They will cause her to weep, out of nowhere, while feeding the jays, or enjoying a Slurpee. They will lead her to gorge on Ben & Jerry's Half Baked ice cream, watching marathons of *Law & Order* and *Snapped*.

She will drive around the backwoods in an endless loop. She will wander through the woods, like her father before her, he who spent an inordinate amount of time out-of-doors, tracking small animals and then blowing their minuscule brains out. She will de-plume dandelions, the childhood jibe coming to mind: *He loves me, he loves me not, he loves me, he loves me not.*

She will neglect her appearance, frightfully so. If he had previously expressed dismay about her lax posture and the stark shade of her lipstick, he would be downright alarmed by her unwashed hair, the forest thickening on her legs, and the hideous splotches on her face.

She will learn everything there is to know about Amber. She will create an electronic doppelgänger who inhabits Amber's Facebook page and keeps track of her LinkedIn profile. She will obtain Amber's high school yearbook from the library (she was, of course, voted most popular, most likely to pursue a career in broadcast journalism). She will memorize the details of Amber's biography in the firm directory (saleswoman of the year, Northeast region). She will learn that Amber participates annually in a 5K walk/run for victims of ovarian cancer; that she purchases her groceries at the Stop & Shop off Route 25; that she takes Pilates classes at Curves; that she shops at Tangiers outlet mall, still apparently able to squeeze into a size 2 junior miss, despite being a full-grown woman with disproportionately large breasts.

The wife will drive in circles, crawl into bed at night, turn out the lights. She will feel the empty space next to her, as if it has mass, as if it is palpable. She will, with the aid of Somnambulis, a nonaddictive sleep aide, fall asleep, remembering nothing in the morn, when the light floods the window and she must once again rise, rise and face the day and the immeasurable emptiness she now feels, the one person in her life who owed her fealty, *gone*.

She will stumble through the day, participate half-heartedly in group discussions on the role of the psychopomp in the harrowing oeuvre, sit sullenly during office hours, return home to her empty house, the one with the flaking cupolas and the dying marigolds in the flower boxes, the building in an overall state of disrepair, structurally unsound, and hope that no one disturbs her as she watches *Hoarders*, contenting herself with the knowledge that she, at least, has not started an unwitting avalanche of household items—the tendency to hoard said to be probative of deeper psychological problems, the need to grasp on to something, *anything*, even if it might be a hideous frog purse, purchased secondhand, or a beat-up Madame Alexander doll in a moth-eaten costume.

She will have a glass, or two, of middling Shiraz; she will stare out of the window. She will vow to lose ten pounds, to trim her split ends, to take care of herself. She will resolve to do something productive, to grade the mountain of papers piling up on Dante's *Inferno*, to take a hike through the woods, to learn to cook spaghetti *alle vongole*, to have a dinner party where perhaps she might invite colleagues in the literature department, and, in a gesture of goodwill, the husband and his new love interest. *She's so progressive, so secure and self-assured*, they would say admiringly. *She's not even remotely threatened!*

One night, as she drives around town (she is, she suspects, figuratively tracing the descent into Hell, round and round, endless circles), she drives by Amber's bungalow. The husband's Audi parked in the driveway, immediately behind her Fiat. A lawn sprinkler refreshes the green grass, a metronomic *thuk, thuk, thuk*. The shutters are open—open!—inviting any passerby, any voyeuristic nut or estranged spouse—to just peek in. Amber gives him a snifter of Dewar's; he accepts. She massages his shoulders from behind, bends down to whisper something in his ear. Life transpires on slow dissolve.

He downs his snifter of whiskey. He rises and takes Amber

by the hand, leading her into the bedroom, somewhere the wife cannot follow, at least not without exiting the vehicle, stealing around the back of the bungalow, and hiding in the rhododendron. The wife will wait, half an hour, an hour, before he emerges, giggling, naked, to procure some ice cubes from the ice-maker. *Clink, clink.*

The wife will turn the engine over, driving, headlights off, away from the scene. She will vomit curbside, then drive straightaway to the 7-Eleven. She will clear the freezer of Ben & Jerry's Half Baked, purchase a peel-top sour cream dip. The rest of the night will transpire in a blur. The world shifts on its axis. The husband is gone, like her mother before, *gone.* He is inhabiting another woman's bed, making ice cubes in her freezer.

The wife rocks in her mother's rocker, driving a groove into the floor. Sometimes she curls up in a ball on the carpet, hugs herself tightly, fearful she will dissolve. She cannot believe that the husband has moved into Amber's bungalow, directed that his mail be sent across town. She cannot believe that he has emptied his drawers, that he has dismantled and taken with him the lifelike anatomical models he uses for trade show demonstrations in lieu of cadavers, the ones with lifelike skin and proportional organs. *Retractor, blade, piercing cut.*

14

I learned to conceal myself. I confined my observations to the late night and early morning hours, when the neighbors were snacking in front of the television or snoozing and uninterested in the investigations of a lonely voyeur. I dimmed the headlights, hiding in the shadows.

I invested in a seat warmer. I overcame my initial embarrassment peeing into small containers. Night after night, I recorded my observations, three pages on average (*Amber clears table; husband takes out the garbage* or *Amber retires early; husband watches porn on the computer; Amber grooms Lulu, the long haired Chihuahua hua*—more attention lavished on the five-pound ball of fluff than ever was paid to me during my turbulent childhood), more knowledgeable about your schedule, your habits, your everyday life, than you. My eyes gradually adjusting to the darkness.

Amber suffered miserably during menses. She gained five pounds of bloat. She stared at the mirror in disbelief at the extent of acne eruption. Sopped up the oil with medicated pads, slathered on benzoyl peroxide, and tried to conceal the pustules with layers of makeup. *You're ugly*, she said to the mirror. Disbelieving in her beauty, or the illusion of it.

Naked, her imperfections were evident. She had stretch marks on her buttocks. The left breast was slightly smaller, deflated. Her eyebrows were dyed to make it appear as if she were naturally honey blond. Her unexpectedly hairy legs necessitated shaving on a daily basis. She burned the bikini area with hot wax and depilatories. I took some comfort in her imperfections, in the notion that she, like the rest of us, was a mortal woman, prone to cyclical bloating and skin eruptions. I rejoiced in these faults, in the recognition that none of us is perfect, none of us so irresistible that she is beyond criticism, capable of withstanding the glare of a magnifying mirror. Up close, the view is never flattering.

The underworld is a dank and dark place, a place where no light penetrates. It is a pit, an abyss, a place of torment and never-ending punishment.

The fetid bog of the irredeemable.

15

It was important to demonstrate to the world that I was getting on with my life, going out, socializing, engaging in normal human interaction.

I recognized that certain behaviors, viz., peering into your shutters, staking out the bungalow, documenting Amber's routines, might be misinterpreted, construed as obsessive or even criminal. The world frowned upon those who peered where they ought not to peer and rummaged through personal effects and eavesdropped on exes, documenting same in spiral-bound notebooks.

I was not inclined to confide in others, to reveal my innermost feelings. I had no confidante, no girlfriend who was the living repository of information concerning ex-boyfriends and ex-husbands and sexual experience levels and the like.

I was, however, acquainted with Madge Loomis, who taught freshman remedial writing. She lamented the dismal state of education these days—students' inability to form a grammatically cogent sentence, to express an idea in an original way, to expunge *like, uh, whatever,* from the vocabulary.

Our assigned parking spaces were side-by-side. One night after class, she suggested, *à l'improviste,* that we go out for a drink. Being a college town, there is no shortage of pubs, taverns, and watering holes where one may imbibe spirits, drink oneself into a pleasing numbness, perseverating until alcoholic blackout.

We ended up at Paradise Lost, near the tracks, a place popular with inebriated collegians and aging bikers alike. In the Hudson Valley, we have many ex-hippies, aging radicals, former bicycle gang members, sixtyish men and women who prance about with faded skull and bones tattoos and full sets of dentures.

Madge's drink of choice was Long Island Iced Tea, a hideous mix of rum and Coca-Cola. I stuck with whiskey, straight up. Madge marveled that I could choke down glass after glass of the "hard stuff," as she put it, shaking her head in disbelief. She recalled an instance when, as a teenager, she had drunk half a bottle of tequila. When, vomitus still in her mouth, Eddie LaBruta fondled her.

I am not an avid conversationalist. I have difficulty discussing others' adolescent traumas, their small-scale woes, their fermenting grudges. *I can't even look at tequila! Or crème de menthe! Once I puked an entire pitcher of Melon Balls! Did you ever try those?* Still, I did my best to appear cordial.

Madge had not had much luck with men. From Eddie, it had all gone downward. A descent, a dizzying spiral. *Nowhere to go but down*, Dante remarked to Virgil. Down, down, falling through the air where the lustful specters float, longing for their corporeal selves. Sinking through the ground where the vain are piled up, rotting, no longer able to gaze upon themselves.

Richie, her current beau, was chronically unemployed or underemployed and, in any event, leeching off her. Madge's elbow slipped off the bar.

"Bringin' on the Heartbreak" was playing on the juke box. We had both of us grown up in the eighties. Electronica, drum machines, "99 Luftballons." The interregnum between the classic rock masterpieces of the seventies and the arrival of grunge in the nineties. I try to block the era out of my mind, not the least because my mother was by then gone, the soundtrack to my woe not the soulful Billy Holiday, or the angst-ridden Nina Simone, but drivel like "Every Rose Has Its Thorn."

"Forget about Eddie," I suggested.

"Here, here." We clinked our glasses.

"I'm sorry, I didn't mean to spill," Madge said. I could already see that I was to be the designated driver, the responsible party, the one who would drag her out at the end of the evening, after she had thrown herself inadvisably onto one of the aging biker types congregating around the pool table.

After Mother left, I was forced to cook and do the house-

work, to learn to make do with canned produce, to mop up
after my father when he collapsed on the floor, drunk yet again.
I learned the ins-and-outs of hangover remedies (lemon juice
to neutralize acid). I learned that *I* was the only one who could
be unfailingly depended upon.

"Are you having fun?" Madge slurred.

"In fact, I am," I said, motioning to the barkeep to fill up
my glass.

"I'm really glad you came."

"Me too," I replied sheepishly. Truly, I was. If not for the
kind invitation, the impromptu suggestion to *Get drunk!* extended in the faculty parking lot, I would have remained shuttered
inside, rereading email correspondence, beating myself up for
being over-the-hill and less-than-desirable. Instead, I was going
out, consorting with others, learning about the biker counter-
culture, getting on with my life.

"You've got to get out there!" she exhorted me. "Take a
chance! Your life isn't over yet! You're still young!"

Sadly, we were not still young. Forty had passed. Paren-
thetical creases had formed around our mouths. Our youthful
skin was becoming dry and flaky. Hairs, intractable hairs, were
popping up in unspeakable places. Hairs so resilient heavy-duty
tweezers were required to uproot them.

We were desirable, perhaps, to a fifty-five-year-old. To an aging biker with a social security check and Medicare. To a retired
state government worker with a pension who'd lived with his
mother for most of his life. To the reclusive Bobby Archer who
lived down the road, squirrel shooting for fun.

"Are we still hot?" She jabbed me in the ribs. "What do ya
think, huh?" Madge spun around on her bar stool, nearly falling
off. The bikers obliged us with a wolf whistle.

"See," Madge said, vindicated. She leaned in, whispering,
"We've all been a little worried about you, honey. We know this,
uh, has been hard on you. Just know you're not alone."

Were they discussing me in the faculty lounge? Pondering
my fate over limp Cup O'Noodles soup? Debating my future

as they wheezed sad, watered-down coffee from the thermos? *There she is, alone, puttering around the old, broken-down Victorian. Alone, while her husband* (you were still my husband, in the eyes of the law) *pranced around town with Amber, by all accounts, "a hot number," "wowza."* Even my supporters were forced to admit that any objectively sane man, given the choice and the opportunity (ample opportunities, sales calls and conventions and product demonstrations), would choose Amber over me.

I winced. I recoiled from the arm she threw around me in a show of camaraderie, solidarity, sister-to-sister support.

"Have a good cry. Let it out," she encouraged me. "You're with friends."

I resisted the invitation to let it all out. I do not like to make a spectacle of myself. I do not like to unburden myself, to reveal my innermost secrets. I am of the view that what is not spoken of does not exist, at least not outside of our tortured, obsessive minds, and thus have adopted strict non-disclosure policies about personal matters, ex-lovers, soon-to-be ex-husbands, estranged mothers, and the like.

I tried to steer the conversation back to Madge, back to her childhood traumas, her repressed memories of Eddie (the mind will bury what it does not wish to dig up, particularly where alcohol and numbing agents are involved). Thankfully, we grew up in an era where inadvisable sex could just be glossed over, forgotten about, where we could wake up caked in vomit, dust ourselves off, and return home, none the wiser.

There are those who believe trauma should be addressed. That we must forgive, but not forget, if only to escape the undertow, the swirling currents, of years of abuse or neglect. But there is a reason we forget. A reason why we drink ourselves into a stupor, why we aim for drunken amnesia, why we prefer to leave the past unexplored, hazy, shrouded in fog. There is a reason we respectfully decline to discuss our problems.

After four Long Island Iced Teas and a shot of tequila, Madge could not remember what she had just said, allowing me to escape the confessional.

"We should do this more often." She elbowed me.

"Yes," I concurred, as she slumped onto the bar. I positioned her head to the side so that she could breathe.

I stared out the window. The rustling shadows, the impossible-to-fathom night. The human heart, an impenetrable place. Lucifer's heart is a frozen chamber. His eternal companions the traitors Cassius and Brutus. For there is no greater sin, no worse offense, than to betray those to whom you owe fealty, those to whom you are bound by blood or by vow, whether as vassal or slave or Roman publican.

I settled the bill and dragged Madge out of the premises. I stuffed her into the back seat of the Volvo, trying not to startle her. We were off, traveling down Route 25 into the ever-deepening darkness. Lucinda Williams clicked on as soon as I turned the engine over. The soundtrack to my despair. I drove with one arm, kept another on Madge so as to prevent her from rolling off the seat.

Driving around town, night after night, week after week, I knew intimately the curves and angles of the roadways, the shoulders and the gulches, the places one is likely to slam into a guardrail, the stretch of rural highway, just outside of town, where one wrong turn can catapult you seventy feet into a ditch. Roaming around after dark, speeding along straightaways, as if daring fate to take me. *Whew, made it around the curve, I'm alive!*

Startled, momentarily, by my acceleration into a curve, Madge awoke. She looked around her, stricken. And then fell unconscious again.

My intent was to drive around, enjoying the scenic byways, until Madge awoke from her stupor. To deposit her safely at home, to tuck her in, rolling her on her side so she did not choke on her stomach contents. To thank her for a fun evening. To make instant coffee and encourage her to drink same in an effort to counteract the effects of inebriation. But instead, I drove past Madge's condo development, around the loop, and doubled back, heading toward Amber's.

I slowed down as I approached the cul-de-sac and killed the

high beams. Just a typical night, surveilling my estranged husband and his mistress, watching as they engaged in hanky-panky in the living room, shutters wide open, not a care to who might be watching outside with high-powered binoculars (available for $49.99 at the Spy Shop). Watching as they blithely groped one another, chased one another semi-naked around the living room, and retired to the bedroom.

Given the number of drinks consumed over the course of the night (*Drink, drink!*), bladder control would prove difficult. My quota of small containers would soon be exhausted. Madge would bolt upright, looking for the nearest toilet, a patch of secluded weeds where she could relieve herself.

Watching as the husband emerges from the bedroom, stark naked, to fetch a glass of ice water. Watching as he contemplates the contents of the fridge—the rabbit food Amber likes to snack on; soy and wheatgrass antioxidant smoothies in their plastic-domed containers—trying to decide what to do. Wasting energy, shifting foot to foot. He could never decide, could he? Always wavered before all the options. He reaches in, grabs a Snickers from behind the head of kale. A single, contraband bar. Stuffing it into his mouth, careful to turn the wrapper inside out and to bury it in the garbage, there to molder among the compostable rot. He shoos away the Chihuahua, *not now, Lulu*. He'd never wanted a dog, had rejected the wife's pleas to adopt one, saying they were too much trouble.

Watching as the husband wanders over to the living room (the bungalow has an open layout, allowing for unimpeded views). Naked on the sectional, he reads the paper. (The *Post*. He has it delivered, now that there is no principled objection.) He moves his lips when he reads. He lingers over the scores, the ongoing tallies, the statistical compilations. He shifts, scratching himself. He seems at once so familiar and so unfamiliar. The past lives on, an alternate version, a different arrangement of atoms. In this version, the husband and the wife live happily ever after, watching reruns of *Hoarders*.

What lives in our hearts, our thorny hearts, is known only

to us. What we keep mum, what we choose not to disclose, what we selectively divulge, the interior closed loop. We can only make surmises, hazard guesses, apply our tired psychoanalytic theories, in trying to divine the true intentions of others. In trying to ascertain why, one day late in January, the husband left. Why, after slathering peanut butter on toast and trimming the edges, the mother jumped into a waiting Cadillac, never to return.

The husband opens the window. He inhales the fresh air, stares into the black beyond. He does not know the wife is out there (she has anti-glare binoculars, for total concealment). He does not know that she is watching him, that she is aware of his comings-and-goings, of his television viewing habits, of the secret places he has stashed his junk food. She is attuned to his moods, to the changes in his demeanor, even more so now, when she is not blinded by her own participation in events, but is merely watching him, a nonparticipant. Though she is sitting surreptitiously across the way, watching events unfold through high-powered binoculars, she feels connected to him, more strongly than when they were living together, there in the crosshairs of lies and warped versions of the truth: *You're just being paranoid, I am not having an affair, lots of people call the wrong number, hanging up without leaving a message.* She feels she knows him, truly knows him, the unvarnished self, the unmediated self, the self that putters around and scratches his balls and stuffs his face with chocolates, the self who enjoys Snickers (much to the chagrin of Amber, who prefers blanched peanuts), the self who is dejected, at the end of the day, questioning his life's purpose, the self who wonders whether there is something beyond peddling medical supplies, inserting catheters into verisimilitudes of the human body.

My observations end midsentence. The husband returns to sleep just after one in the morning, after reading the sports page and stuffing his face.

"Where the hell are we?" Madge bolted awake.

"Nowhere," I assured her. "Just stopped for a pee." I started the car, anxious to get away. I did not want to blow my cover. I did not want to be seen as a crazed voyeur, an obsessive ex-spouse, someone with nothing better to do than to eavesdrop on the lives of others. I did not want to be seen as the type of person who would purchase high-powered binoculars, a deranged observer obsessed with documenting every detail of my husband's new life, recording every moment, chronicling what he did when I wasn't there, so that in some sense, some warped, maniacal sense, I could continue to share his life.

I took a sharp turn at the end of the street and headed back on Route 25, the wind rustling through the window.

Marge rubbed her eyes and sat up. "Did we go home with those guys?" she asked, stricken.

"You mean Zeke and Rob?" I asked, watching her face in the rearview mirror. Their names had somehow escaped her, despite hours of drunken bantering, recklessly hurled darts, and promises to keep in touch.

"I guess," she stammered.

"Sad to say, they were bitterly disappointed that we declined their offer to go home with them." I had not sunk so low that I would accept any drunken lout's offer to ride his motorcycle, that I would jump on the chance to exchange bodily fluids in the alleyway outside the bar, even in my battered, semi-functional state.

"They were nice guys," Madge recalled wistfully. She had escaped with her dignity intact. Left with a telephone number, instead of a venereal disease. She had flirted and bantered, rather than fornicated in the bathroom stall on excrement-splattered porcelain. All-in-all, a good evening.

I deposited Madge at her condo. Back to her life with Richie, the sporadically employed carpenter who spent his days watching *Wheel of Fortune*, his nights drinking Heineken, perpetually exhausted from filling out resumes and updating his profile on LinkedIn.

"We should do it again!" she said, brightening. She stumbled along the cobblestone path, disappeared inside. The number of Zeke written on the back of a matchbook and stuffed into her bra.

The mother left one day without explanation. For all intents and purposes, she had ceased to exist. She was no longer part of their lives. *She might as well be dead,* the father said. *Then at least I could claim her social security benefits.* The mother became fixed in time, the mother circa 1979, with plaid pants and a macramé vest, the mother who had a copy of Erica Jong stuffed under her pillow. These were the details from which she was to construct her, or reconstruct her, to try to ascertain her intent. The *why.* The moment when discontent, malaise, and garden-variety boredom coalesced, the moment when she gave herself permission to leave.

16

My father was a tinkerer. A man who fiddled with spare parts, a man who constructed transistor radios out of busted circuitry and leftover bits, a man who spent most of his time in the cellar, calibrating vises, rather than upstairs with his wife and young daughter, at least purporting to communicate.

We were, for most of my childhood, lacking in resources, desperately poor, getting by but just barely. My mother worked as a substitute teacher. Her sporadic earnings, together with those from my father's salvage operations, sustained us. Enough to fill a cabinet with nonperishables, to keep the refrigerator stocked with beer, to maintain the line on the gas gauge at half-empty. My mother packed my lunch every day—a peanut butter sandwich, cut on the diagonal, with the crusts trimmed. Left notes tucked in the corners of my aluminum lunch box, *I love you, peaches. You can do anything!* Evanescent reminders on lined white paper. Notes I crumpled up and stuffed in my pockets, lest my classmates read them and subject me to even more strenuous torments. My father was of the view that my mother coddled me, sparing me character-building assessments of my worth and value as a human being.

One year, my father having received a sum from the sale of a patent, we went on our one and only family vacation. A road trip, in the old station wagon, to the shores of Lac des Pins. In those days, no passport was necessary. Border control consisted of a smile and a wave on through, not the meddlesome baggage checks and intrusive drug-sniffing canines of today's paranoid world. I had never been on a vacation. I had never ventured outside the town limits. For all I knew, the world was bounded by the glade, stopping abruptly at the old rail line.

Vistas opened before me, the horizon ever receding, as we

traveled, in our gas-guzzling Ford, along the highways and by-ways of our neighbor to the north. My mother had relatives in Newfoundland, second and third cousins we intended to look up on our journey. But we never knocked on those doors. We rented a cabin on the shores of the lake, a rustic A-frame with wood beams and gingham linens. I spent weeks going through the cabinets and the wardrobes, discovering notes in the strangest of places (*Ne touchez pas, SVP*). The occupants had gone elsewhere for the summer, presumably somewhere balmier and better for the sinuses.

Father had no cellar to descend into, no dank place where he could brood, be alone, and chain smoke.

Mother left her collection of 45s at home. She was relegated to listening to the Pelletier's transistor radio, which picked up Radio France from a ham operator out of Montreal. My mother and I found an old dollhouse. Remarkably like our own Victorian, with cupolas and a flaking roof. My mother dusted it off and set it up in my room. Every day we would enact domestic scenarios in miniature: the doll children waking on the upper floors, the doll mother frying eggs in the kitchen (sunny-side up eggs in a tiny cast-iron pan), the dog begging for a scrap (a bowl with *Fido* painted thereon). The doll mother waving them off to school. "I love you, Ophelia." Words that issued so easily from her.

We ate meals at the round table with the captain's chairs and the gingham tablecloth, the only memory I have of us together as a family, laughing and bantering and interacting in socially appropriate ways. Mother gazing at Father, flirting, a gleam in her eye. *You're a rascal, my word.* Father pulling her closer, inhaling her scent, sunshine and butterscotch, the only time I remember their bodies intersecting, interlocked, hand in hand, and arms around each other. I vibrated with joy; I was attuned to the *timbre* of their happiness, the knowing gazes and the playful whacks, the groans of their bodies entwined on the old featherbed. The child who feels secure in her parents' love, who believes in the fortitude of their marital bond, has no reason to believe that the family will not go on as before, no reason to believe that the family qua family will cease to exist.

I spent long days on the shore of the lake, basking in their shadows, Father reading Wittgenstein or Schopenhauer, Mother embroidering, absentmindedly humming—a tune that eludes me now, a tune I hear only in fragments, lost to the erosion of time and memory. I made sandcastles, using the plastic trowel and buckets the family of the house had left behind (*pour l'enfant*). Hard-packed walls around the castle to stop the inflow of water. A moat to protect the castle keep. An elaborate system of fortifications for a structure that was made of sand, that could wash away, and did one night during a violent thunderstorm, a thunderclap and an inundation, and afternoons' worth of architectural planning come to naught.

One day, out on the lake, I became distracted by a dragonfly skimming the water—its wings a brilliant, heartbreaking blue. I leaned to the right, unbalancing the canoe, and the boat capsized. The waters were not rough, but they were deep, an unfathomable distance. I remember sinking, giving in to the sensation, down, down. A commotion ashore, as my parents, long shadows, paddled toward me, frantically, trying to reach me before I disappeared into the murk.

She already knew she was leaving. She knew when Father pulled me from the water, gasping for air; she knew when we were sitting around the gingham table, laughing; she knew when we were traveling north on the interstate. She knew watching me build my sandcastles; she knew wiping away my tears, explaining that nature is random and destructive. She knew watching fireflies skimming the water, glimmering in the darkness. She had already made the decision. She had already chosen the trajectory. Her path would diverge from ours, continuing onward, elsewhere. She wanted to savor one last time together, as a family, before irretrievably smashing it all to pieces.

17

I receive emails from would-be suitors, correspondents enamored of a jailbird, soon-to-be-parolee. Men who promise to be the man you could never be, to be the lover I deserve. Men who express wonderment at my ability to subdue two medium-sized captives. Men who suggest I tie them up and whack them with a shovel. Men who propose marriage and woo me with princess-cut cubic zirconia. *Will u be mine? I promise to love u 4ever.*

One promises to be the Paris to my Helen. To take me back to Cincinnati, where he will ensure that I am treated as I deserve. He has a disability pension and an eye, it appears, for a reasonably attractive woman of a certain age. *You are beautiful,* he writes, seeing beyond thick spectacles and ill-fitting orange jumpsuit. *I would never leave you,* he assures. *Be mine.*

18

MARCH 2011

I went on a blind date with a friend of Madge's. A professor of accounting and actuarial sciences. A man fascinated with the probabilities and the statistical chances of death. He drove an Acura, a consistently high performer in crash safety tests. He avoided two-lane highways, lonely country roads, anywhere a distracted or sleepy driver might drift across the median, leading to a head-on collision. Victor opined that as a single, childless woman in my forties, I had virtually no chance of remarriage, or of giving birth to my own genetic offspring. I would, however, make an excellent neighbor (childless singletons known to be social, to bring banana bread to elderly shut-ins), and pet owner (nine out of ten childless singletons own one or more cat; a whopping five out of ten own three or more).

As the child of two brooding depressives, one of whom had manic phases (flights of leave-taking, never to return), I had a 75 percent chance of suffering from a similar malaise and debilitation of the spirit.

As an academic in my forties, I stood no chance of making tenure or even of weathering the next round of budget cutbacks.

I nodded, taking all of it in.

"Is your portfolio diversified?" Victor asked me. He was invested in all sectors of the economy, insulating him from precipitous shocks. He had cash reserves in the event of a catastrophic market event or a fluctuation in the price of commodities.

"I'm not very market savvy," I confided, inviting a lecture

on cyclical bubbles, real estate busts, and inevitable market corrections.

"Mortgage-backed securities," he harrumphed. "I never believed in them."

I nodded and smiled nervously. I drank three glasses of pinot noir. He drank exactly one and a half glasses of cabernet. Any more, he counseled me, would exceed the daily recommendation for heart health and predispose one to alcoholism.

"Do you have a cat?" he asked.

"No, not as of yet," I laughed.

"Interesting," he said. "Statistically aberrational for your cohort."

"Although I'm thinking of going to the animal shelter this weekend. In between frozen dinners."

He did not laugh. He never laughed. Human behavior can be predicted to an astonishing degree, he assured me. Ah, Victor, on this I have to disagree. There is always an anomaly, a statistical fluke, a small percentage of cases who remain unaccounted for, whose behavior defies all predictive models. No regression analysis, no actuarial voodoo, can predict their behavior to within a reasonable degree of certainty.

19

Victor and I went on a second and third date. As a divorcée, I scored higher on measures of commitment and companionability than those my age who had remained defiantly single. More likely, in other words, to cling to a man in desperation, to view him as the antidote to loneliness.

As expected, Victor was an unimaginative lover. Someone who insisted on keeping his socks on. Someone who vigorously flossed and gargled afterward. Someone who startled when I called him a *bad boy*. Someone who was content to snuggle.

"How long have you been separated?" he asked, padding around naked, inspecting the contents of my refrigerator.

"Five, six months, I don't know."

"Hmmm. Once parties have separated, the likelihood of a reunion is nil. Especially if there are no children." The beer foamed over the edge of the can.

The estranged wife, the soon-to-be divorcée, will entertain Victor, cook him a meal once or twice a week, invite him into her bed, enduring less than satisfying sexual relations. *See, she is getting on with her life! She is living, once again! She is having an orgasm at least intermittently.*

The estranged wife will claim to be infatuated. She will return Victor's calls promptly, lest he think she is uninterested; she will stock her pantry with Honey Crunch granola, his preferred breakfast cereal, demonstrating that she is thoughtful, attentive, willing to make accommodations.

The estranged wife will attend events hosted by the Department of Accounting and Actuarial Sciences. She will feign interest as the department chairman drones on about the *Laffer* curve. She will impale mini-cocktail franks on plastic toothpicks, dip them in mustard, and pray that someone will kill her before she is subjected to another speech on the LIBOR index.

Though she is standing by Victor's side, holding his hand, feeling his breath upon her neck (frequently stale due to salivary gland insufficiency), she has the sense none of this is real. Though he refers to her now as *girlfriend*, rather than friend, or companion, none of it registers. Though he has mentioned the possibility of moving in, or at least keeping a drawer in the bedside table, she feels nothing. She has no comment. She walks through life, disbelieving.

There is another life, elsewhere. A life more real than the one she is pantomiming with Victor, the professor of actuarial sciences. A body more palpable than the one she wakes up next to, three nights out of seven, the one suffering from night sweats and restless leg syndrome. A man more vivid, more real, than the one sitting at the breakfast table, glowering over the stock market reports.

On the nights Victor is away, she wanders. She drives the byways, the darkened back roads, the black stretches of macadam. She listens to Lucinda Williams, over and over again. She has taken up smoking, like her mother before her. A nervous habit, something to do while she is parked on the corner, watching. She inhales a lungful and exhales tiny, perfect rings, smoke signals, spent carcinogens. Life gone off on a tangent, in another direction, splintered off.

20

I remember the night you proposed. I was thirty, an age when a woman has begun to think about the quality of her ova, about mutual fund diversification, about the prospect of being alone for the remainder of her years. (I was not yet aware of the existence of my half-siblings, living a parallel life in a bungalow in Pensacola, Florida, they who would sell their stories to the tabloids, purporting to know me, or at least be related to me, so as to profit off the lurid elements of this story. But alas.)

It was a night in late summer. A muggy, insufferable night, the only thing between us and molestation by the *Aedes canadensis* a mesh porch screen. You were always sensitive to the mosquito, your blood an aphrodisiac. *Damned mosquitos*, you'd glower.

I sat next to you on the porch swing. The crickets singing, the mosquitos enjoying their last hurrah before flying into a mist of nerve toxin. Your arm around me, pulling me in, whispering in my ear, *I love you. Remember, I love you*, my mother uttered before slipping out of town with the Cadillac salesman, exiling herself from my life. *I love you, Ophelia.* Though it is customary to reciprocate, with at least a *me too*, I found myself unable. It wasn't as if I didn't love you; indeed, I loved you even more than you loved me. And yet, the words, the articulation of the feeling, the expression of the inner sentiment, did not come easily. A lifetime of tamping down one's feelings will have this effect.

I smiled, cupped your face in my hands. As much feeling as I could muster. I must have mumbled the words. I remember feeling them, like an electrical charge. *I love you, Andy.* There are gaps in memory, ellipses, lacunae in which we can [insert] what we presume to have been said. *I love you, Andy.* You put your head on my lap. I stroked your hair. A tender gesture. Your eyes blue in a certain light, green in another. Your hair thick, with impossible to tame cowlicks.

You know, I've been thinking. Maybe it's time we ought to be married. You're not getting any younger, you know. The air crackled.

You had not yet purchased a ring. You were not bent on one knee, as in traditional depictions of the act of proposal (your head on my lap, the porch swing creaking). And yet I could think of no more romantic gesture—there, enclosed in the porch, where no mosquito could touch us, mar our happiness with itchy welts.

Yes, I replied. *Yes.* And in that moment our bond was soldered. An understanding that you would always be there for me, and I for you, lest death or catastrophe intervene. We would remain faithful to each other, never looking upon another, until we slipped the mortal coil. A bargain, a pact, a sacred bond.

21

April 2011

One night, shortly after having warmed up chicken à la king in the microwave for Victor, he inquired, mid-mouthful. "Did I see you on Willow Street last night?"

"I don't think so," I replied. "I was grading papers." I was not the best liar; I preferred to lie by omission, to escape in the ellipses, rather than affirmatively misrepresent (a significant legal, if not moral distinction). "Well, maybe," I backtracked. "I did go to the mini-mart for some milk. Why?" I inquired. It is best, when confronted, to go on the offensive, the better to distract from one's transgressions. I learned this from you, during the course of many fraught denials, soliloquies about insidious, unfounded accusations and the perils of my jealous nature.

"I just could have sworn I saw you parked on the side of the road."

"Don't think so," I said, vigorously scrubbing the bottom of the pan. "Well, could be. I might have paused to change the radio station. I don't like doing that while driving."

"Maybe I was just imagining it," he mused, shoveling another spoonful into his mouth.

"Seems so," I concurred.

Had Victor seen me? Parked on the side of the road, peering into your shutters, recording observations in my notebook? I wasn't entirely sure. The possibilities endlessly refracted. A hall of mirrors, catching us at unexpected moments, betraying angles we'd never before contemplated.

I took precautions. I effaced all traces of the Saratoga College decal from the rear window. I took to wearing a tousled wig.

I abandoned the Volvo by the side of the road, positioning myself high in an elm in the woods behind Amber's bungalow (my father had taught me the art of concealment, the art of hiding inside oneself). From my perch, I could see everything transpiring within. Watching you, recording your movements.

I needed to know what had become of you. To confirm that you hadn't been involved in a highway pile-up or drunken accident, that you were not lying in an emergency room under the sobriquet John Doe, that you hadn't suffered traumatic amnesia and were wandering, somewhere, along the Eastern Seaboard. I needed to know that you were all right, that no harm had befallen you, that you had returned, safe and sound, from your sales tour of the Northeast region. I needed to assure myself that you still existed, somewhere, even if that somewhere were not with me, even if that somewhere was a bungalow at the end of Willow Street. That you hadn't disappeared, never to be heard from again (at least not until overwhelmed by stage IV cancer and treatments so cost-prohibitive your family members were obliged to reach out to abandoned daughters to fill in the gap). Etcetera, etcetera.

Some wonder whether I wasn't torturing myself, watching you night after night, recording every moment of your life apart from me. I would pore over these entries of surreptitious surveillance in search of a clue, something to explain why you had left, why you had chosen to forsake our lives together for one with Amber, an explanation beyond the obvious (physical attributes, the allure of youth and vigor). But from these pages, hundreds in total, this covert chronicle of your life apart from me, little can be discerned beyond mundane cliché and tiresome recitations of nighttime television viewing rituals: *Amber and Andy watch marathon of* The First 48, *snuggling on the loveseat. Amber fails to cover her mouth when picking kernels of microwave popcorn from her teeth. Amber worries about Lulu the Chihuahua choking on a kernel.* Little can be discerned of the heart, the repository of emotion, unable to survive an hour or two beyond clinical brain death, becoming rapidly ischemic. Does he think of the wife, of the one he has abandoned? Does he adhere to the principle *out of sight, out of mind,* or does he live in the past, inhabiting the empty spaces, what persists in memory, long after the *actus rea?*

Andy and Amber watching Cops. *Andy massages Amber's back, delivering karate chops to the scapula. Amber appropriates the choicest morsels in the moose mix, the chocolate-covered bits and the almonds, leaving him the unpopped kernels and some ground peanuts. Bedtime at eleven. Andy attempts to initiate lovemaking but is rebuffed.*

22

The prison psychiatrist speculates that I suffered a break from reality, that I was living in a fantasy world, a world defined not by any realistic parameters but by unsubstantiated and demonstrably untrue versions of reality. She speculates that I was in a dissociative fugue state for most of the period, accounting for the gaps in my memory. She believes me to be a neurotic manipulator with obsessional tendencies intent on controlling every aspect of my environment.

The prison psychiatrist maintains that it is unhealthy to eavesdrop on one's ex following a breakup. One can never achieve closure, it appears, when one is skulking about, hiding in the trees, overhearing conversations one is not intended to overhear (my lip-reading skills on a par with those of a hearing-impaired individual), witnessing scenes to which one ought not to be privy. One can never move on when one is obsessively recording the ex's movements, hiding in the bushes, instead of getting out there, burnishing one's online dating profile, accepting the fact of loss.

We explore the ways I might have dealt with loss in a healthier manner. I might have kept a journal, a safe place wherein to give vent to feelings of hurt occasioned by your betrayal. I might have put our wedding album in storage, instead of poring over it nightly, reliving our first moments together as husband and wife, our first bite of cake, our first dance to "You Light Up My Life."

I must give voice to feelings, instead of allowing myself to be consumed by venomous rage. I must learn to accept others' decisions, even if they negatively affect me and cause me eviscerating pain.

The only way I will heal and move on, truly move on, is by acknowledging the gaping hole in myself, the suppurating wound, the one that has festered in the darkness, lo these many years, and to reclaim my agency, refusing to cede to others the power to reject and blindside me and erode my self-worth.

Imagine Amber is seated before you, the prison psychiatrist instructs. (I'm growing tired of this routine. The imagined interlocutor. The virtual interrogation.) *Tell her what you want to tell her. Tell her how she's hurt you. Say, how could you do this to me?*

I conjure Amber from memory. The one or two occasions I'd seen her up close, in three dimensions. Her angles softer than I'd imagined, teeth less blindingly white, voice not a high-pitched squeak but unexpectedly lower in register.

He's mine, Amber, I manage. *He's mine.*

It is uncharitable, perhaps, to be arguing with a dead woman. To impugn her memory, resurrect her for gestalt role-playing.

Go away, I eke out. *You have no right.* I follow the psychiatrist's directive to take my anger out on the supportive foam pillow.

You're not that pretty, I say, perhaps unfairly, to she who in her last minutes had been reduced to a slobbering, snot-streaked mess, every trace of makeup effaced.

I stop mauling the pillow. It is unfair to be pummeling the late Ms. Halloway, even symbolically via the stand-in of a therapeutic foam pillow. But for me, she would be here. Living, respiring, raising funds on behalf of victims of childhood cancer. But for me, you would be a productive member of society, not a traumatized individual with a mild speech impediment (temporal lobe damage) and rancor in your heart. The camera loses focus up close; the subject dissolves around the edges.

23

I vowed to try! To open my heart to the possibility of falling in love with Victor, or at least relaxing my resistance to a deeper commitment. To accompany him to faculty events without wincing or bristling at the sobriquet, *girlfriend*. To engage in sexual relations with him twice a week, the average number of times for an adult in a committed relationship. To nestle in his arms afterward, offering a complimentary *that was nice*, or *you make me feel so good*, even if I felt like howling and running away. Such would be proof positive that I had moved on and was not unduly fixated on you and your tart of a girlfriend.

I made Victor my specialty, spaghetti *alle vongole*. We raised a toast to ourselves, so lucky to have found each other at this stage in our lives. I held his hand across the table and watched as he slurped the spaghetti, trying to convince myself *it's not so bad*. I wiped the corner of his mouth, an unexpectedly tender gesture. I told him I was happy to have found him, the most forthcoming I'd been in three months of courtship.

Victor scooped me up in his arms. He told me he had *feelings* for me, to which I nodded vigorously. I encouraged him to undress me. I was wearing the crotch-snap teddy. I had gone for a wax at the day spa, anticipating close scrutiny of the region.

I allowed him to ravish me. I ground myself into him, arching my back, instead of lying there stoically. I might have encouraged him to *fuck me*. I might have said *harder, ram me*, wanting him to fill my inner spaces. The void, the place where no light shines. I bit my lip, shuddered inwardly. I experienced release, a long, moaning *decrescendo*. I did not immediately disengage myself, but nuzzled in the pit of his arm. I gazed into his eyes, pupils wide in the darkness.

"You're full of surprises," Victor said, brushing the hair from my eyes. Statistical anomalies fascinated him. Data that could not be reconciled with the trends; skewed distributions that defied easy explanation.

"You're just getting to know me," I teased. The wind chimes accentuating the off-beat. One-TWO.

On this, Victor, I fear, I was entirely *as expected.* The rebound relationship is doomed to fail, statistically speaking. Even in cases where the wife is not driving by the ex's house and watching him through high-powered binoculars. Even when she is not fantasizing about harm—an unforeseeable accident, an unsightly skin condition—befalling his new girlfriend.

24

I accompanied Victor to the convention of professors of accounting and actuarial sciences in Myrtle Beach, South Carolina. While he attended seminars on topics like G.A.A.S. and G.A.A.P., I frittered the time away at the pool, sunning my pallid skin and sipping mai tais. At any hour of the day or night I could order a turkey club, merely by dialing *3 and communicating with the wait staff. *Crisp bacon please and mayo on the side.*

The king-size bed enabled me to sleep in peace, avoiding unwanted incursions, be they restless legs or somnolent embraces. *I'm exhausted after a day in the sun,* I groaned, when Victor returned from the conference and attempted to initiate lovemaking.

I'm on vacation! See me enjoying myself!

When we returned to New York, Victor said we ought to have a *talk.* I bristled. I hated talks, discussions, airings of mutual grievances. What begins as a forum for open communication, for improving relations, for joint decision-making, inevitably ends as the means for imparting disastrous information. *I thought we ought to talk about it first, but I've made up my mind, I'm leaving. By the way, I never loved you.*

I wandered upstairs and began unpacking. In my experience, it is preferable to avoid unpleasantries, to dodge rancor. Ill feelings will dissipate over time, or at least become less potent.

"Did you hear me?" Victor followed.

"I heard you," I mumbled.

"I don't understand you," he said, not the first time I had been accused of being opaque, less than transparent, withholding in the extreme.

"Are you listening?" he asked.

"I'm listening," I assured him, as I resumed unpacking, unwrinkling dresses and putting them in the wardrobe.

"What do I have to say to get through to you?" He grew exasperated. He shook his head and paced back and forth, hands in pockets, turning them inside out, finding them empty. "I feel like I'm talking to myself sometimes." A stunning insight for someone who lectured to bored undergraduates for a living.

"Well, you're not talking to yourself. I'm here," I said. "Would you please move aside so I can put the suitcase back in the closet."

"Give me the goddamn suitcase," he huffed, wresting the overnight case from me. "I'm trying to talk to you!" he sighed. "Sit down," he said. "There's just no easy way to say this."

As suspected, he did not wish merely to talk. With fanatical, bullet-point precision, he reviewed the course of our relationship, from blind date to present. *I had reservations about dating a recent divorcée, but I grew to be quite fond of you. You never complained about going to the faculty get-togethers. You forgave my stodginess. And you can be lovely. The* alle vongole! He swooned, bringing fingers to his lips. He removed his glasses, looking at me slightly off-center. He was cross-eyed. I had never noticed it before. *But it seems to me*, he continued. *It seems to me that this is not going to work out.* I shirked from physical contact. I seemed to just *endure lovemaking.* I hadn't given him any drawer space. Three months had gone by and I was still reluctant to acknowledge him publicly, let alone embrace the commonplace descriptor, *boyfriend.* It seemed to him that I was not invested in the relationship; that I still had feelings for my ex; that I was incapable, yet, of loving someone else; that I was stuck in the past, a recursive loop; that his heart would be broken if he remained with me.

I nodded. I could not take issue with anything he had said. I had been marking time with him, stumbling through the measures. When interrogated regarding my well-being, post-breakup, I could say, *I'm seeing someone,* and be done with the inquiries. When questions surfaced about my mental health, my inability to move on, I could shrug it off, mention that I had given Victor a drawer in the wardrobe.

"I'm sorry," I offered. For truly I was. I had underestimated his affinity for me. Trampled upon his feelings while attempting to discern my own, opaque intentions. I had led him to believe he and I wanted the same things from life, to wit: love, companionship, a mildly satisfactory sex life.

I cried for myself. For what my breakup with Victor portended. My inability to bond with another human being a certain signifier that I had not *moved on*, but was hopelessly stuck. Mired in the past, unable to accept that you had forsaken me. Others would no doubt seize upon the rupture to paint me as a delusional, obsessive woman with no intent of putting the marriage behind me.

"I know." Victor squeezed my shoulder.

"I guess you'll be going then," I said.

I did not embrace him. I did not bestow one last, tepid kiss upon his lips. He had already been written out of my life. An undeveloped theme, a passing note. I heard his Acura (the highest-rated performer in crash safety testing) turn over and drive away, his tires gnashing the gravel.

Students of the mind (psychologists, psychiatrists, armchair therapists) speculate that we are bound to reenact certain conflicts, that certain dramas will replay themselves in our lives, over and over again, a theme with infinite variations. Parents scar us in profound and imponderable ways with their casual disparagements, their disdain for our very person, their sullen absences, reverberating throughout the rest of our lives. The psyche, imprinted by trauma, is never again the same. We develop unhealthy stress responses, we learn to distance ourselves from unpleasant realities, we learn to dissociate, to invent fictions, rather than to accept unpalatable truths: *Your mother left you for a Cadillac salesman. Your father believed death preferable to a long coda in the attic room. Your husband no longer loves you, if ever he did.*

25

The house next to Amber's went into foreclosure, an unexpected lucky turn of events, at least for me. I wriggled into a basement window, the only one that had not been boarded up by the sheriff. (A technical trespass, I admit, but who was I trespassing upon? Mr. Lark had quit the premises after falling behind on his mortgage payments, and the house had yet to be resold.) I was able to watch you for days on end, now that I didn't need to void into small containers or remain perched in a tree.

I purchased a telescope, which I smuggled in through the window in parts and assembled thereafter. I could train my sights on any room in the house, not only living room and kitchen but the bedroom where you and Amber slumbered (you in boxer shorts; she in garish thong and matching balconette bra from Frederick's of Hollywood). I watched you and Amber showering in the morning through a fogged-up window. I saw you dutifully flossing and brushing your teeth. You gargled, committed to the fight against gingivitis and plaque build-up. I watched you on the toilet, absentmindedly thumbing through magazines and picking your nose.

I watched you day in, day out (longer on weekends, not having even a semblance of a social life to intrude). Scarfing down granola in the morning and eating pad thai for dinner. Sharing moose mix on the couch. Bathing Lulu with hypoallergenic shampoo and brushing her shiny coat.

You chased after Amber and tackled her in the bedroom. You liked to rip off her underwear with your teeth. You spent hours making love, hours during which I'd absent myself mentally, relegating the proceedings to a darkened cubby. Hours during which I distracted myself by reciting *The Inferno* in the vernacular, *Da questa tema a ciò che tu ti solve, dirotti perch'io veeni e quell ch'io ntesi nel primo punto che di te mi dolve.*

You made love to Amber every day, sometimes twice a day. Your repertoire included not only the *splitting of the bamboo*, but *crouching tiger.* I watched you bend, and yield, and contort yourselves into unfathomable positions. I watched you sweat, exude your essences, and in the end collapse into her arms. You and Amber had been cohabiting four months, assuredly long enough for malaise to have set in. And yet you continued to ravish her night after night, showing no signs of boredom or *rallentando* of your passion.

I closed the viewfinder and curled into a ball. Howled as loudly as the suicides in the seventh circle, not that anyone would hear me. I was entombed in a basement, only a tiny window onto the light.

26

MAY 2011

Amber returned late one evening after a night of debauchery at Rummy's Paradise (or so I surmised from the discarded leaflet on the front lawn, *Ladies Drink for Free!*). She was too inebriated, apparently, to fit key into lock and fell asleep on the doorstep. Finding her there, miniskirt askew, Mardi Gras beads strung around her neck—on the whole not a picture of responsible adulthood—you had a fit. You pulled her inside by one arm, like a caveman. She startled awake, murmuring a stream of non sequiturs, nonsensical phrases from which I made out the unmistakable name Josh. Josh! A reference to her barroom beau? To an old flame who still occupied her mind? Someone whom she still evidently held in esteem, particularly when drunk and unable to censor herself.

"Josh? Who's Josh?" you echoed, apparently drawing the same conclusions as I.

"Come here," she said, trying to pull you closer.

"You make me sick," you said, wriggling free of her.

Amber cried. She wheedled. She cajoled. Even the least gifted lip reader could make out that she was *sorry*, she had *made a mistake* and *it'll never happen again, baby, can you find it in your heart to forgive me?*, sobbing and hiccuping throughout the apologia until finally she passed out on the carpeting. You left her on the floor and returned to bed, never once checking on her to see if she was all right, if she had gagged or choked on her own vomit.

I had difficulty sleeping (Mr. Lark had ripped up the carpeting, exposing the warped and rotted floorboards underneath, part of his campaign to thwart the bank and diminish the resale value of the home). I watched you pace back and forth, fume and curse under your breath, until at last you collapsed into bed. You slept like a baby. You always had. *Why do you need sleeping pills?* you'd ask me, failing to understand that depression, all-consuming worry, and hypervigilance induced by wondering whether your father would put a bullet through his brain, as threatened—conspired to make some of us insomniac wrecks.

Had you tired, finally, of Amber? Now that you were co-habitating, rather than renting a room at the Minnie Ha-Ha, were you growing bored with her? Now that you slept next to her, fighting for bed space, instead of cuddling for a minute or two post-coitus, was your relationship suffering? Now that you shared a bathroom and saw her scrubbed clean; now that you saw the true state of her hair—not smooth and soft, but a frizzy, untidy mess she spent hours blowing into place—were you still enamored of her? Did the sight of her send you into a sexual frenzy, or had desire been dulled by proximity, the many rude encounters of daily life?

I lay awake all night, contemplating the possibilities. (My sleep further marred by thieves scavenging upstairs for copper wire, anything that might be salvaged and sold for a profit.) You might pack your bag in the morn. Return to me with your sample cases and your head hung low, saying I had been right about Amber, she really was a tart, a tart who danced on bars and flung Mardi Gras beads and on the whole did not exhibit the best judgment. You might beg my forgiveness, ask me for another chance, say you were sorry you had walked out on me, suggesting a second honeymoon—a Caribbean isle, perhaps, somewhere with warm trade winds and calypso music. We might try once more to have a baby, for surely I could endure the hormone treatments with you by my side to help me deal with the mood swings. It was not too late. We were still married, still officially bound to one another, enjoying reciprocal rights of dower and inheritance. (My parents technically remained married, even after my mother cuckolded my father with the Cadillac salesman and bore him three illegitimate children. Children who were, officially, my father's offspring, for a woman's husband is the presumed father, regardless of what is true and demonstrably to the contrary.)

But, alas, come the morn you had forgiven Amber. Made her your famous hangover remedy, grapefruit juice and cayenne paper, said to clear the mind as well as the sinuses and to alleviate the inevitable hangover headache. Toasted two slices of white bread, trimmed the crusts, and sliced them on the diagonal. Swept up the purple and green beads underfoot. Helped Amber to the table, firmly supporting her so she did not stumble or crash. Told her that you loved her, despite her obvious faults. Said you were in it *for the duration*, kissing and nuzzling her, though she had yet to brush her teeth or to rinse her vomitus spewing mouth.

There are things that are inexplicable, beyond our capacity to understand or to endure. I closed the shutter over the lens of the telescope and curled up in a ball on the floor.

27

Father encouraged me to look upon my mother's leave-taking as a survivalist exercise. I learned to boil wa ter. I developed a taste for Hamburger Helper. I avoided my father from the hours of six until midnight, when he drank most prolifically. I conjured the image of my mother as I lay in bed at night, her features etching themselves in memory, as assuredly as if she were still there, hovering over me, trimming the crusts on my peanut butter sandwiches. Her eyes changed shade depending on the light. Blue or green, or blue-green, a watery hue. There was peach fuzz on the side of her face. Her reedy voice, so full of air and light; *I love you, Ophelia*, she said more frequently in the day than my father managed to utter in a lifetime.

Bob's Cadillac Emporium shuttered soon after her departure. Someone purporting to be Bob's wife knocked on our door one night, demanding to know where they had gone to, cursing my hussy mother for stealing her husband and leaving her with three unruly boys and a lot with no resale value.

My father slammed the door in her face, saying he didn't want to be disturbed. (He never wanted to be disturbed.) He declined to comment on rumors that my mother had run off with Bob, occasioning closure of a business that had been in the family since the dawn of the Cadillac. We avoided passing by the shuttered dealership, lest my father be reduced to a fit of swearing, vituperative commentary regarding his fickle wife and her penchant for hucksters.

One day I espied a crumpled-up envelope in the trash. It bore the postmark Pensacola, FL. Somewhere I could locate on a map. Someplace with coordinates, a discernible latitude and longitude, average climate seventy-five degrees. I imagined her living in a white clapboard house with a picket fence and magnolias (the state flower).

When my father was in one of his sullen rages, I'd threaten to go to her. *I know where she is*, I'd glower. Start to pack a suitcase. Sit on the creaking porch swing, awaiting the Greyhound bus. It traveled along the Eastern Seaboard, stopping at Philadelphia, Washington, DC, and other destinations, before arriving in the panhandle. I only had to endure twenty-four hours in a bus with forty other passengers, marking the miles, holding my bladder between rest stops.

"Have a nice trip," Father said.

28

I was running low on provisions. Gallon jugs of water to flush the toilet. Ten-hour energy drinks to keep me awake during the long hours at the watch. A rain slicker, to help repel the drops of water infiltrating through the roof, where Mr. Lark had taken to the shingles with a pickax, hoping further to reduce the resale value of his home.

I decided to slip out during the afternoon. The window had become stuck during the two or three days I had been sealed inside. It was with great effort that I succeeded in pushing it open and in wriggling through its swollen frame. Amber's Chihuahua yelped mercilessly at me as I scurried across the back lawn and into my vehicle. The Volvo had been plastered with fliers and ticketed (establishing, beyond a shadow of a doubt, that I was in the vicinity on or about May 26, 2011, helping to establish a "course of harassing conduct," and upping the charges).

It was the end of the term, the end of the school year, and the end of us. I was overcome with feelings of loss. I failed to yield at the merge and was run aground on the side of the road. There, I rested my head against the steering wheel, trying to collect myself (I was not "banging" my head against the wheel, as some who have watched the surveillance tape from the convenience store claim, but merely composing myself after what was, after all, a minor traffic mishap).

I did not think to call a friend. I did not think to unburden myself, to talk it through, and thereby be reassured of my ultimate worth as a human being. Misery is not to be shared with polite company, or with family members, who would in any event be indifferent to our plight. I continued on until the juncture with Route 25.

Had watching you, day in and day out, granted me special

insight, enabling me to predict your next move before it was even made? If only it were so.

I was relieved to be at home. I sat on the porch swing, remembering the eve you had proposed, the rustling wind, the cicada's song, the searing zap as the short-lived *Aedes canadensis* met its fate. We return to these coordinates, times that for us hold the most meaning. Our first loves; our first realization that Mother had, in fact, left us and was not merely on an extended tour of historic homes of the Hudson Valley (my father on the telephone—with whom?—saying she was gone, she had done it this time, goddamn her to Hell).

I emptied the bug zapper. They never tired of hurling themselves against the light, of flying straight into mists of nerve toxin, not content until they had self-destructed. They had failed to adapt, falling still for the lure.

The mail had piled up everywhere. Junk mail and credit card statements and supermarket circulars. At the bottom of the moldering pile, beneath a free coupon for a French manicure at the nail salon in the strip mall, I espied it. Securely stapled to blue card stock. The caption typed in. *Andrew Fairweather, petitioner, versus Ophelia Fairweather, respondent, for a judgment and decree of divorce.*

The estranged, soon-to-be divorced wife sinks to her knees. She rains fists upon her head, as if she can jar herself into a different reality. She finds the only item of the husband's remaining in the house, a large stuffed bear—now that she thinks of it, he probably won it at the carnival, spurred on by Amber to sink the basket or to whack the mole, rather than, as he claimed, bidding for it at children's cancer charity event—and rips the stuffing from its innards. Sinks her fingers into its guts and disembowels it. A carnage of cotton batting in the living room.

The estranged, soon-to-be-divorced wife knows she cannot contest the evidence. She cannot, like a fifties housewife, refuse to grant the divorce, insist that the husband remain with her for better or worse. She cannot invoke church or state of the well-being of their never-born children. She cannot refuse to cooperate with the so-called referee, refuse to turn over financial records by the date designated in the papers.

She has no ability to alter the inevitable outcome.

29

The prison psychiatrist speculates that receipt of the divorce papers triggered a break with reality. That upon reading your complaint in consecutively numbered paragraphs, the wife—already depressed, heartsick, dealing with compound traumas—snapped. The mind can only endure so much before the psyche, unable to cope, engages in imaginative reinvention, fine-tuning of reality, selective excision of those elements deemed unduly distressing.

I consulted an attorney, a specialist in family law, on behalf of an unspecified friend who had been served with divorce papers. I posited, hypothetically, how said friend may or may not have hacked into her husband's email accounts; how she may or may not have "friended" the lover, pretending to be an old school chum; how she may or may not have adopted the husband's online identity for purposes of composing fictitious emails to his lover purporting to break up with her.

According to Saul Rubinowitz, Esq., said friend would be lucky if she escaped without being served with a criminal complaint for harassment and intentional invasion of privacy, both class A misdemeanors under the penal code. She would be lucky to avoid the payment of spousal support to the husband, who worked on commission and therefore had no steady income or at least no objectively verifiable income, enabling him to hide income and assets while pretending to be impecunious. As the higher-earning spouse, she would end up paying his legal fees as well as her own. Each spouse was entitled to continue in the lifestyle to which he or she was accustomed prior to the divorce, regardless of fault, regardless of documented instances of infidelity at the Minnie Ha-Ha, notwithstanding copious emails which left no doubt whatsoever that he and his paramour had been engaged in a clandestine relationship for the better part of a year before the wife was forced to resort to electronic impersonation in order to terminate (or purport to terminate) the affair.

"But he's a proven adulterer!" I protested.

Here, Rubinowitz, Esq., informed me that fault was no longer relevant. The New York State Legislature had seen fit, in recent years, to move away from fault-based grounds like *adultery* and *constructive abandonment*, toward a more congenial mediation-based model. A friendly, court-supervised division of assets, culminating in a decree mutually satisfactory to both parties. The adulterous spouse no longer forfeited, by virtue of his iniquitous activities, any and all claim to the property of the other. There was no stigma attached to consorting with your mistress at the motel pool or fornicating with her in the marital bed. The law no longer saw fit to punish what the counselor-at-law called "human frailty," activities like meeting with your hussy every Tuesday and Thursday at the Minnie Ha-Ha.

"I have to say, I'm quite shocked." I coughed into my fist, shifting in Mr. Rubinowitz, Esq.'s chair.

"Got to move with the times. What can I say? These adultery cases used to clog up the system. Turned the divorce trial into 'gotcha,' with spouses trying to catch one another in the act."

The law used to strong-arm adulterous spouses into reconciliation, lest they expose themselves in court to salacious accusation and risk walking away with nothing. Now, with the liberalization of Article 10 of the Domestic Relations Law, you had nothing to fear from rumors that you had been consorting with Amber. The evidence I had collected—the guest register at the Minnie Ha-Ha, where you and Amber signed in as Mr. and Mrs. Smith (a handwriting specimen!); the push-up bra I had found in your car, stuffed under the bucket seat (double DDs!)—irrelevant as far as the court was concerned. Adultery had been decriminalized in the interest of streamlining our system of justice and eliminating the stigma attached to cheating spouses.

"My fee is $450 per hour. Should your friend wish to retain me."

"You've given me a lot to think about." The scales of justice were tilted in your favor.

I thanked Saul Rubinowitz, Esq., for the legal education and said I would be in touch.

My head was reeling. How was it possible that fault played no role in divorce proceedings? That a marriage could be dissolved merely by invoking *irreconcilable differences?* You could break my heart and profit handsomely thereby. You had leverage to demand alimony payments. You were no doubt massaging third-quarter sales figures in an effort to underrepresent your income and gain the impecunious advantage.

I went to the college to retrieve employment and financial records that would prove relevant to any impending division of assets. The deed, which conclusively demonstrated that the house had been bequeathed to me by my mother, and thus qualified as "separate property" insulated from the claims of ex-spouses.

Madge Loomis, my newfound friend, noticed me brooding in the faculty lounge. I am not an easy person to read. I have deficits in communication and interpersonal skills. I have difficulty unburdening myself, even in the presence of someone who has opened up to me, confiding her most intimate secrets, tales of questionable drunken sex, probable gang rape, whilst drunk in a low-rent bar.

"You can talk to me," Madge prodded.

I hesitated. What for others is part of natural social intercourse, *How are you? Well, that's too bad about your cocker spaniel having mange, call me if you need anything, I'm here for you*, is for me an awkward and excruciating exercise, accustomed, as I am, to never being taken into account, to being ignored, encouraged to actively suppress my feelings, whatever they might be.

"Is it Victor?" She looked at me. "I'm so terribly sorry." She shook her head. "I knew something must have happened when I saw him at the faculty party with someone from the anthropology department. Don't be sad." She smiled. "You two are just in transition periods. You weren't meant for each other. He's too stuffy." She wrinkled her nose.

I nodded, looking down. I was content to let the misunderstanding lie, to let her believe that I was distressed by my recent breakup with Victor—we had, after all, dated for three months, even if the relationship had never made a mark on my psyche—rather than confessing the sordid truth. To wit: that I had taken up residence in the soon-to-be foreclosed-upon property next to Amber's, that I was watching your every movement through a high-powered telescope, that I was making surreptitious friends with Amber's Chihuahua, hoping to lure it to my side, that I was lying in the darkness in stress positions, night after night, obsessively recording my observations in consecutively numbered notebooks, wondering what had become of our life together.

Madge flung an arm around me. "You'll find someone who will be your perfect match. You'll see. Victor's a Virgo anyway," Madge said. "They're too uptight."

Having had no close childhood friend; having had, in the years after my mother left, only a mongrel stray and a wounded bird for company, I was not accustomed to these rituals of friendship. The reassuring hug, the placating *there, there.*

"Thank you, Madge," I said. I knew enough to pantomime the responses of a normal human being. Maybe I could fool others into thinking that I, too, was a normal human being with a normal range of emotions and at least a negligible ability to express my feelings in a constructive manner.

Madge looked at me the way one looks at a puppy who has had an accident on the carpet. *What, oh what, are we to do with you?*

30

I took a break for a few days and watched a marathon of *Hoarders* on the Arts & Entertainment channel. There is always someone more deranged than we, someone with over four hundred Tupperware containers or glass zebras or souvenir toothpick holders who insists she does not have a problem (or at least not one beyond the capacity of seven dumpsters). Someone with a dead cat in the crisper drawer. Someone who cannot bear to let anything go, not one of the dozens of potholders, or frayed sock puppets, or Betty Crocker cake mixes she intends one day to bake (should she ever locate the oven under the box of childhood mementos, the belongings of the long-dead child or grandchild to whom the hoard is an unwitting tribute).

At the end of the week, I resumed the watch. Entered under cover of night, through the basement window; made friends of some mongrel cats who had taken up residence there. I stunned Lulu the Chihuahua by throwing a twig at her head, momentarily stopping the incessant yapping.

I adjusted the viewfinder on the telescope and peered inside: the furniture in the same arrangement. The museum prints on the wall. Monet, Manet, water lilies, sunflowers. One of the less unsettling Picassos—cubist instruments—nothing maimed or decapitated or juxtaposed onto something else entirely.

Did the prospect of impending divorce in any way affect you? *The marriage shall be dissolved as if the parties had never been joined.* (This, from Article 10 of the Domestic Relations Law of the State of New York.) As if the parties had never known one another, as if they had never shared the same bed or hiked together in the Shawangunks, helping one another navigate the rock face. As if they hadn't explored every inch of one another, run their fingers over scars too deep, too embedded to comprehend, remarking upon the other's resilience and impressive scar tissue formation. As if they hadn't been joined together in the presence of God and two witnesses, during a brief ecumenical service (your parents questioned whether you weren't rushing into things; my mother was wasting away, somewhere, in the presence of my three half-sisters and the husband who would never be her husband, only the verisimilitude of one). As if they hadn't lain together, night after night, watching the rise and fall of each other's chests, listening to the rumblings of their internal organs. As if they hadn't spent five years together in the crumbling Victorian, sharing the same utensils, consuming the same mineral-laden tap water, for all intents and purposes one. As if she hadn't served as his surgical dummy, allowing him to practice on her exposed abdomen, to indicate, with indelible marker, where to make the incision so as to better visualize the organs, where to position the laparoscope so as to minimize the trauma. *Go ahead and slice me open*, she said, pressing the trocar into her belly.

You did not seem in any way to be affected. You went about your normal routines, waking at the same hour, going to bed at the same hour, eating the same granola cereal with the same five sliced strawberries. You had, I realized, already written me out of your life, already decided upon a different future. You had already embarked on a new storyline, one that did not intersect with mine, save for some nettlesome details like the partitioning of marital property and the filing of one last joint tax return, to ensure that we were taking mutual advantage of all available deductions.

Indeed, you appeared to be *elated*, lighter in step, inclined to spontaneous frolic, your face no longer creased with worry, or darkened by some unspecified mood. The proverbial weight, *i.e.*, me, had been lifted from your shoulders.

It was evident that you regarded me the way I had regarded Victor—as someone inconsequential, someone with whom to pass the time and to enjoy a quick, generally silent breakfast, someone with whom to be mutually aghast at hoarders who risked burial under an avalanche of their own belongings—but someone who had never registered, someone who had never made a groove in the soul.

I should have walked away then. I should have dismantled the telescope, emptied the small containers, and abandoned the watch. I should have left the crawl space to the feral cats and the nocturnal foragers. Brushed my hair, burned my fetid sweatpants, and gotten on with my life, availing myself of on-line dating services as dear Madge had urged me (*I can help you with your profile!*). I should have quit the Lark property, once and for all, and not just whenever the bank inspectors appeared. I should have dealt with spousal abandonment as my father had before me, choosing never to speak of the matter and ignoring legal process whenever it appeared in the mail (in those days one could not simply obtain a divorce after the passage of six months, no questions asked, but needed the assent of the wronged party to tear the union asunder).

But it was already too late.

31

You and Amber disappeared for the weekend. I watched you go. You scolded Amber for overpacking and smacked her on the rear. You leaned in to give her a kiss. You said you couldn't believe how lucky you were to be *so in love*. You had never felt *so alive*. You lifted her up and carried her into the car...Audi ahum. You backed out of the driveway and disappeared around the corner.

I found myself unable to breathe. Growing dizzy, light-headed, unable to trust my perceptions. The world inside a basement is dank. The walls cold, the air stuffy, the cobwebs prolific.

I awaited your return with a family fun size of kettle chips and a jar of sour cream dip. I passed the hours curled in a fetal position, reliving scenes from our marriage—the vista from Skytop as you proclaimed your eternal love for me, the copy of *Gray's Anatomy* you gave me for my birthday, trying to educate me regarding the veinous byways of the body, the means of establishing guidewire access. You promised we'd have a baby one day, once the doctors gave us medical clearance, assured us that benign tumors wouldn't crowd out any developing fetus, choke him of a food supply.

You'd left the Chihuahua in an outdoor enclosure, food pellets delivered at timed intervals from a chute. The pet yapped and whelped. My nerves were fraught (an abandoned house, alas, is filled with souring odors, rotting floorboards, the droppings of opportunistic animals). I was beset by the musings of an overactive imagination. I was contemplating the two of you soaking in a heart-shaped tub, lolling naked in bed, engaging in frenzied sexual intercourse over the course of the next forty-eight hours.

"Please shut up," I hissed at Lulu.

She startled at the mention of her name. But then the plaintive whimpering, *I'm all alone, please save me, no one is here to scratch behind my ears or to give me a gourmet doggy treat.*

I slipped outside and made my way to her enclosure. She whelped, pressing down pathetically on the button that released food into the chute. "No more," I said, turning my palms up, the universally understood sign for *I have nothing, go away and stop pestering me.*

"Is this what you want?" I dangled a strip of beef jerky above her head.

Perhaps the olfactory incitement was too much; perhaps, alone in the yard for two days, no one to pet behind her ears or to give her a belly scratch, she had grown lonely; perhaps, never knowing when duck liver pâté might arrive from the chute, she had grown aggressive, maniacal, broken by lack of sustenance and abrupt withdrawal of affections. Perhaps I should have simply allowed her a bite of the jerky, rather than wresting it from her jaws just as she, starving and shivering from the rain, was about to devour it.

She bit me viciously, sinking her teeth into the soft flesh of my arm and leaving a bloody imprint.

"Look what you've done! You hurt me! You stupid animal!" I warned Lulu, in no uncertain terms, to stay away if she knew what was best for her. I told her to keep her distance, to stick to the perimeter of the yard, to forage for whatever worms or grubs she could find.

But she wouldn't listen. She continued to growl, to make it be known that she was not happy I had snatched the jerky away. She continued to yap at an unnerving pitch, threatening to rouse otherwise complacent neighbors.

"Shoo," I hissed, trying to shake her off. "Shoo, be gone," I reiterated. She was a spoiled creature, one who couldn't be content with gourmet kibble or the thousand square feet of outdoor space she had been given. One who needed to be petted all the time, scratched on the belly, told *good doggy.*

"Go away," I glowered. My arm was smarting, the wound festering, bits of skin hanging off.

She was taunting me with her glossy coat, her bright shiny eyes. Reminding me, with her imperious and objectively outlandish demands, of the unfairness of the world. I would need to irrigate the wound and to apply salve lest I develop a suppurating infection. I'd have a scar to attest to the fact that I'd been mauled by a four-pound purebred with malice in its heart.

I grabbed the nearest object. To wit, the chute programmed to deliver doggy pellets at timed intervals. Stainless steel, scratch resistant, guaranteed for life. Wielding it as best as my injured arm would allow, I brought my club squarely down on the toy breed's tiny skull (mass times surface of an object equals greater force).

She crumpled to the ground. Twitched a few moments, before falling silent altogether.

Animals have no souls, or so they tell us.

I stood above the lifeless body. It was too late to scratch behind her ears and suggest that we could still be friends. I felt like a fraud contributing to the Humane Society, passing myself off as a champion of the animals, having inflicted blunt force trauma on an innocent house pet. She did not deserve to die, to be silenced forever with a decisive *thwack*. Like me, she had been left to fend for herself, to go it alone for long intervals, and was at the mercy of capricious parents, albeit ones who left her with gourmet treats.

I debated whether to bury her in the shallow fill, near the property line, or whether to roll her in a blanket and dispose of her in the town dump. I couldn't leave her remnants for the nocturnal foragers to pick over. Using a shovel that I found in the garage, I dug a hole near the tree line. Placed her gently therein. Murmured a prayer for her eternal repose.

May the souls of the faithful departed, through the mercy of God, rest in peace. Amen.

The prison psychiatrist speculates that I transferred my rage toward Amber onto the toy breed, that in assaulting the four-pound purebred I was, in essence, giving expression to a deeper rage I felt against its owner. The prison psychiatrist imagines that watching you and Amber day in and day out, watching your relationship develop and deepen over time, witnessing the warm expression of feelings, *I love you, I love you, too, I'm so much happier now*...had given rise to a murderous rage, a groundswell of anger, that I had no socially acceptable way of expressing.

The penalty for inflicting battery upon a household pet is surprisingly lenient—a class E misdemeanor, no worse than driving with a broken taillight. Hurting a defenseless four-pound animal did not reflect well on my character, however, and in all likelihood was responsible for turning some of the jurors against me (juror #5 was observed to wear a T-shirt with an ironed-on photo of an Irish setter), mitigating against any natural sympathies they might have harbored for me as a jilted and wronged wife. No doubt certain jurors believed shoving a lifeless canine's body into a hole in the ground to be a cold, calculated act. If I could cover up the death of a helpless toy breed, letting the world believe it had simply run away (Amber posted fliers throughout the neighborhood, promising a reward for its return), then I was indeed capable of anything.

If I may say a word in my defense. There is no showboating prosecutor trying to advance his career by railing against a killer of defenseless purebreds. There is no judge shouting *order* and admonishing me to *get on with it* before the end of the next century.

There is only me, alone in my prison cell. I do not deny that there might have been, in the words of the prison psychiatrist, some element of *displaced rage* involved. I am not, however, a person who enjoys inflicting cruelty on animals, just because she is bigger and controls the doggy treats. I have always loved animals. I have always loved the innocent, the blameless, and the pure of heart.

32

I marked the passage of time by tracing grooves in the wood floor: one week, two weeks, three weeks. I was suffering from lack of sunlight, from Vitamin D deficiency, from an irregular sleep schedule (up all night; sleeping while you and Amber were at work), from the destabilizing effects of confinement in a boarded-up house, no one to talk to save an old shrunken head that I had found in the basement.

Would you like some tea? It is a pleasant afternoon, isn't it?

I'm sure you must have interesting adventures to recount. I've been boarded up here so long, I could use a diversion,

I'm afraid all I have are some barbecue potato chips and a Ding-Dong I haven't been able to make regular trips to the Stop & Shop. We can share.

I developed tunnel vision, an inability to see beyond the sights of the telescope. My eyes suffered fatigue from staring at a fixed point. From failing ever to adjust the focus. *Observations* spilled into the seventh volume.

33

I return, again and again, to this theme of abandonment. Mother left without a word of forewarning, or at least an ominous chord change signaling the act of leave-taking, *I'm so sorry, but I have to go, I will think of you always.* She deprived me even of this, of the final goodbye, of this small acknowledgment, *life as you've always known it will change, remember to eat your oatmeal every morning.*

I am left with a half-eaten sandwich, cut on the diagonal. Scattered crumbs on the table. *Remember, I love you.* The clack of the screen door. Steps echoing down the path. The smooth seal of the Cadillac as she got in and shut the door, never looking behind, never so much as a postcard, *thinking of you* or *still alive* or *guess what, I've had three more children.* Even in the face of her own imminent death, she found herself unable to reach out, to call, but left the awkward task to her three other daughters, the ones she chose to stay with, apparently believing motherhood to be a selective enterprise, rather than a lifelong commitment.

Left without the benefit of an explanation, a relevant tidbit, *your father and I just aren't getting along, it's not you,* something I could hang on to, averting thousands of hours of feckless speculations, wondering why, thinking she might return if I left everything just as it was, the plate on the table, the jar of peanut butter in the cupboard, a sacred tableau, still life of the mother who left circa 1979, *please do not touch.*

She had run off with Bob, of Bob's Cadillac, to the sunnier clime of Pensacola. She set up a new home, had three more daughters—replacements, I can only speculate, for the one she left behind. Left me alone to fend for myself, there with a father with dubious parenting skills and a shotgun in the garage. Left me to my own surmises as to why she had reneged on her parental responsibilities, chosen Bob over us, driven straight through to Florida, never looking in the rearview mirror.

The prison psychiatrist counsels me to reimagine the past. To return to the pivotal moment, to imagine the dialogue as it should have taken place, *I'm so sorry but I have to leave, I am in love with another man, your father just wouldn't understand.* She has me play the part of my mother, to enable me to see events through her eyes. She has me switch, play the part of my eight-year-old abandoned self, to impress upon me the fact that it wasn't my fault. She gives me a supportive foam pillow and encourages me to take out my aggression against the mother who left, the mother frozen in time. She tells my adult self, the supposedly rational and reasonable self, to embrace the eight-year-old girl, to protect her, to scold the adults who were supposed to protect her but instead failed miserably, viz., yelling at her whenever she inquired after her mother, telling her she was no good, disappearing into the attic with a shotgun.

Say what you want to say to her, she prods me. *She never gave you the opportunity. She left you alone to fend for yourself. Say what you want to say to her now. Why did you leave me? Say it.*

Why, my voice cracks. *Why...* I trail off. A catch in the throat; something that prevents me from full-throated expression.

Why what? the psychiatrist prompts, encouraging me to shade in the picture, to cross-hatch the details, Bob in the driver's seat, telling her to *get a move on,* my mother casting her eyes backward, taking one last look at the tableau, the Victorian and the child she was leaving behind, the sandwich only half-eaten, the calculus laid bare, to leave or not to leave, to start anew or to molder in place.

Why did you leave me? Why?

34

LATE JUNE 2011

Amber plastered the neighborhood with fliers of Lulu. Professional quality photographs of the ersatz pet. A reward payable upon her return, in good condition, not having suffered privations and depredations and of course not having expired from blunt force trauma and being dumped in a hole in the backyard.

She passed the fliers out on street corners; she ambushed people in strip malls as they searched for shopping carts. *Have you seen this dog?* More fuss made over the lost pet than had ever been made over me, abandoned by her mother and left with a father who, in retrospect it is clear, suffered from an undiagnosed mental disorder, accounting for long spells of near catatonia punctuated by days awake in the woods, hunting small animals for sport.

She even intercepted me as I was emerging from the minimart, a quick stop to replenish my supplies of beef jerky and potato chips and to purchase roach motels to mitigate the infestations. I was not looking my best. I had worn the same outfit, viz., sagging sweatpants and a college jersey, for days, my eyes unable to endure the sunlight. Clearly, she had not scrutinized our wedding photograph too closely, else she would have recognized me as your estranged wife, the woman she had cuckolded, the woman whose husband she consorted with at the Minnie Ha-Ha, so frequently as to entitle them to a special rate for loyal customers.

"My dog is lost," she explained. "I'm offering a reward."

"Hmmm." I examined the flier. Lulu was undeniably cute.

If one discounted the yapping and the difficulty sharing doggy treats.

"She just disappeared." Amber sniffled. Her eyes were puffy. Her skin far less smooth than I had imagined.

"I'm terribly sorry," I said, averting my eyes. I twirled my hair, a habit of self-soothing I had acquired during years of maternal absence.

"Thank you for taking a flier. Most people just walk by."

"No need to thank me."

"Do we know each other?" She squinted at me. She was attractive in a way I, with my too-small eyes and fleshy nose, would never be.

"No," I assured her.

I took the flier and thrust it into my bag, along with the chips and the jerky and the gallon jugs of water. The moldering paper, LOST DOG, later introduced by the prosecutor as evidence of malice aforethought, a trophy, like the lock of hair or gold medallion a serial killer wrests from his victims. *Ladies and gentlemen, she knew the poor dog to be dead, and yet she took the flier, rather than flinging it away, as would any sane person...*

She said, I'm sorry you lost your dog, pretending not to recognize the creature, though she had beat it senseless and stuffed it into a hole in the ground.

The encounter with Amber in the parking lot rattled me. Though I had watched her day in and day out for months, it had never occurred to me that one day, placarding the neighborhood with fliers for a lost pet—*cherished dog, please call immediately*—her path might cross mine, that she might return the gaze that had thus far remained one-sided. I knew every inch of her skin: the scaly patch on her shoulder that she loofahed to no avail; the waist bulge she went to pains to conceal. I had seen her pick her teeth and plumb her nostrils and go through boxes of Tampax super-plus protection. And still, viewing her in the real world, out of focus, was unsettling.

I questioned what I was doing ensconced in the basement of the abandoned and soon-to-be-foreclosed-upon Lark property, subsisting on jerky and chips, conversing with a swashbuckling coconut head, watching you and Amber through the viewfinder. I had not gotten on with my life, as others had urged me to do; I was not exploring my options; I was not enjoying the life of a professional singleton (cocktail hours at swanky bars; miniature quiches on silver platters; jazz explorations, every other Wednesday, at Uptempo).

Torturing myself with what-ifs. What if you had never attended the annual convention of guidewire salesmen? What if you had never encountered Amber in the hotel bar, looking *ripe* and *irresistible*?

If Bob had leased space for his Cadillac emporium in the next town over, he might never have crossed paths with Mother, uprooting her from my life, erasing her from my future.

Having emerged from my lair for at least a few hours, I thought it prudent to stop by the attorney's office to discuss the impending divorce proceedings. I had three weeks to respond to your petition, to assert why the parties' marriage ought not be dissolved pursuant to Article 10 of the Domestic Relations Law, to deny accusations, in consecutively numbered paragraphs, concerning alleged electronic eavesdropping and identity theft.

Eschewing a tissue, I proceeded to recount the circumstances surrounding the irretrievable breakdown of the marriage. The affair with Ms. Amber Halloway, medical supplies sales associate. The liaisons at the Minnie Ha-Ha, a family establishment. The overnight "sales calls," purportedly to check on this-or-that disgruntled or dissatisfied customer. The withdrawal of marital affections.

Saul Rubinowitz, Esq., nodded gravely.

Though I no doubt had the superior moral hand, I did not have the superior legal one. The advent of so-called no fault divorce laws had erased any stigma associated with adultery, with lust and marital treachery, enabling parties to obtain a divorce merely upon vague assertions of irreconcilable differences. So long as the parties observed the statutory waiting period—a six-month legally imposed window during which they were to reflect, and to possibly reconsider the wisdom of permanently dissolving their marriage—a divorce could be had upon the flimsiest of excuses.

Proof positive that my husband had been consorting with a hussy did not get me very far. Proof that he had regular liaisons with her at the Minnie Ha-Ha, that the police had been summoned to the scene in response to reports of a disturbance—might give rise to a chuckle, but was ultimately irrelevant to the court proceedings. Proof that he shared Ms. Amber Halloway's bed, that he purchased polyester lingerie for her from the Frederick's of Hollywood catalog, perhaps poorly reflected on his taste and level of refinement, but legally made no difference. The marriage could be dissolved, as if it had never existed, after the mere passage of six months and proof of service upon the respondent.

"First you get screwed, then you get screwed over," as my attorney elegantly summed up. "Listen, are you getting enough sleep? You don't look so good."

Mr. Rubinowitz had the kind of unnatural tan one acquired in spray booths or on electrified tanning beds. The kind of white teeth made only possible by periodic visits to the dentist to bleach the enamel. The kind of suit one bought off the rack, at Joseph A. Banks, during the semi-annual men's sale.

"Spare yourself some angst." He turned philosophical. "Don't fight the divorce. You can't win. You'll just come across as a crazed and desperate wife. Meanwhile, get some sleep. You look like a wreck," he said, no doubt alluding to my pallor, my dark under-eye circles, my unkempt hair, so knotty I no longer bothered to comb through or otherwise style it.

"Yes...thank you," I managed to stammer. It was difficult for me to carry on a conversation. I had for so long been living in the abandoned and foreclosed-upon property, without the benefit of company, of human interaction, no one to talk to save a shrunken head, discussions one-sided. *What do you think of the red teddy? It's rather gauche, isn't it?*

"It's what I'm here for." He smiled, before reminding me about the retainer check. "You should get out there!" he urged me. "Plenty of fish in the sea." He winked. "Divorce isn't the end of the world." Indeed, it was a new beginning. I would no longer have to self-identify as "married." I could check the box for *divorced* or *single*. I had no designated beneficiaries, no one to speak for me were I to fall into a coma or otherwise be unable to communicate my wishes concerning life-extending measures. Having officially no kin, no legal relations, my estate, my deteriorating estate (the shingles falling off, the floorboards rotting) would escheat to the State of New York.

"I'll contact his attorney and get the paperwork in order." He winked. "You'll be better off without him, you'll see."

I caught a glimpse of myself in the mirror. Failing to eat at regular mealtimes, or to enjoy anything approximating a well-balanced diet, I had lost at least ten pounds. My hair hung limp on my shoulders, my ends helplessly split. Blemishes had erupted along the hairline. I had never—not even while composing my dissertation (*Hell's Inner Circles: Notions of Relative Fault and the Scourge of Eternal Punishment*) nor defending it to four academics who tortured me concerning the specifics of the Malebolge—looked so terrible.

"A vacation works wonders," Rubinowitz, Esq., said, seeing me sizing myself up and no doubt coming to a similar conclusion. "A week in the sun, on the beach. Water skiing, or parasailing," he said, overestimating my avidity for new and destabilizing experiences. "There's just one thing," he said, lowering his voice. "Given the, uh, allegations of electronic eavesdropping, no doubt they'll want to get a restraining order. Just stay away from the two of them. Don't give them any ammunition," he counseled me. "What's the best number to reach you?" he asked.

"I'm back and forth a lot," I said, neglecting to inform him that I had taken up residence in the abandoned property next to Amber's, that I might have, on one or two occasions, tiptoed into the house, drunk lukewarm coffee from your mug (*Go, Buffalo Bills!*), eaten the crusts of your charred toast, the plate (Fiesta!, from our wedding registry) still warm. "Leave a message," I advised.

He had another consultation booked after mine and was anxious to usher me out of the office.

35

Though my father had grounds for divorce, viz., adultery, abandonment, he refused to file for one. It was contrary to the edicts of the church he sporadically attended. He would choose to honor his vows, despite the other party's running off to Florida with Bob, of Bob's Cadillac Emporium. He maintained until the end of his days (shotgun aimed at the roof of the mouth; death instantaneous) that he was a married man, precluded from consorting with other women.

My father bought a used El Dorado from Bob the year before he ran off with my mother. He was appalled by Bob's effrontery in seducing and then running off with the wife of a paying customer, in failing to honor the warranty, when, not two years later, the car expired on the shoulder of I-95, the transmission shot, unable to go on any longer.

"Always honor your promises, Ophelia," my father said. "That's what counts."

36

July 2011

Our counselors-at-law scheduled an afternoon session at the house for the express purpose of resolving conflicting claims of ownership to various household effects. The items in dispute included glazed Fiesta!, anodized aluminum pots and pans, and kitchen miscellany. Our lives together nothing more, in the end, than divisible crockery.

I failed to arrive at the appointed hour. (I was surprised at the property by a bank appraiser. He spent an inordinate amount of time snapping photos, taking measurements, while I remained cramped in a crawl space, barely able to breathe. Upon leaving, he reboarded up the door and windows, trapping me inside. I had to tear off the plywood boards, claw the nails off, in order to have a hope of making the scheduled appointment.) Rubinowtiz, Esq., left me several texts, explaining that failure to appear for court-ordered proceedings reflected poorly on me and would in all likelihood be used to extract even greater concessions. What he said, specifically, was: *Get ur ass over here or he and Amber are going to make off with your living room furnishings and the juicer. We r losing whatever leverage we have to keep him from invading your deferred compensation plan.*

I did not have time to freshen up, nor even to dust the plywood debris from my person. "I'm here, I'm here," I burst in.

"It's about time," you grumbled, shaking your head. "Where've you been?" you demanded. "Never mind," you said, "I don't want to know. Let's get down to it."

We were to state our competing claims as succinctly as possible, refraining from injecting unnecessary or inflammatory comments.

"The juicer was a wedding gift from one of my colleagues. She doesn't use it." You pointed at me. "She drinks only coffee."

"Take it," I acquiesced. My gracious rapprochement, unfortunately, did not inspire you to be generous in kind.

"I need the anodized pots. She doesn't cook."

"And you do?" I shot back.

"I cook more than you," you lied.

You staked a claim to the Pottery Barn sofa and loveseat. You said you had no items with which to furnish an apartment. You insinuated that you were sitting on floorboards, eating ramen warmed up in the microwave.

"Now hold on." I reddened. "He's living with, with that—" I stammered. I wanted to say that you were living with the well-endowed hussy who had broken up our marriage, but my counselor-at-law was giving me the death stare. "He's living with someone else, and she has plenty of furnishings, including a matching sofa and love seat (albeit in a horrid chintz) and a breakfast table," I fumed, resenting your insinuation that you were a pauper sleeping on a futon and subsisting on ramen, three packets for a dollar.

"I'm not living with anyone," you baldly asserted.

"Well, where, pray tell, are you currently residing?" I demanded, arms akimbo.

"None of your business," you had the audacity to assert. *None of my business.* You could obtain a restraining order upon one-sided averments that I had stalked and harassed you, invaded your privacy, and caused a scene at the Minnie Ha-Ha (omitting any mention whatsoever of your purpose in being at said motel, in my happening upon you in flagrante delicto, wrapped in nothing more than musty bed sheets); you could demand marital support, maintaining that as a salesman your income was sporadic and subject to fluctuating demand in the fickle market for medical supplies; you could try to force a sale of the house and to make off with half the proceeds—my mother's legacy, the only thing of value she ever left me. Yet I could not question your bona fides in demanding the entire set of anodized cookware. I was not entitled to know where you were currently living, or with whom.

"You have a lot of nerve," I asserted. "Here." I dislodged a wall-mounted picture of the Bavarian Alps you had once professed interest in. "Why don't you take this too? You just want to bleed me dry."

(And you accused me of a lack of emotion! Of being an emotional flatline, a cipher, frustratingly nonresponsive.)

"You don't even need the furniture. You have a perfectly comfortable matching set from Huffman Koos," I proclaimed, revealing the likely provenance of Amber's furnishings. "You have a cast-iron skillet, for God's sake." (And a juicer, and an espresso/cappuccino maker, and pewter bar accessories.)

"How do you know that?" you asked. "How would you know what I do or do not have?"

"Just hazarding a guess." My counselor-at-law was frantically hand-signaling me, pantomiming self-strangulation, a gesture generally understood to mean *say no more, shut up now, you're only hanging yourself.*

"You'd better not be following me," you asserted.

"God, who's paranoid?" I shook my head, doing my best to appear unfazed. I had pried apart plywood and crawled out a window in order to be on time for our court-ordered assignation. I had spoken to no one but a shrunken head for the preceding three days. I was unaccustomed to conversational give-and-take, to up close, flesh-and-blood interactions.

"I'm warning you, Ophelia. I've already had to change all my passwords. The stunt you pulled posting Amber's photographs. (Acting on a whim, I had, perhaps inadvisably, uploaded your cache of naked and semi-naked photos of Amber to a website where jilted lovers posted photos of their exes.)

"We've already stipulated to drop those allegations," my lawyer interjected, having engaged in protracted negotiations to erase the more disturbing particulars from the public record, allegations of electronic impersonation and gross invasion of privacy and photoshopping of body parts.

"I'm not following you," I asserted. Though I had, that very morning, watched you enjoy a bagel slathered in cream cheese. Though I had watched you bestow a peck on Amber's cheek, and embrace her tenderly, before driving to a cadaver simulation.

"Just look at you." You shook your head. "You're a mess." Spending all the days indoors, no sunshine to lift my spirits, no one but a shrunken coconut head to talk to, I no doubt suffered from Vitamin D deficiency, from spiritual malaise, among other things.

"Just get on with your life. This fixation is unhealthy."

"Don't flatter yourself," I seethed. "You're not exactly a prize." You might have been uncommonly handsome, charming, even, but you were dishonest, disloyal, and had difficulties remaining financially afloat even in the best of times, when guidewire sales were at an all-time high.

"Consider yourself warned," you glowered.

In the end, you walked off with the juicer, the cookware, and the sofa (you had rented a U-Haul, evidently anticipating a favorable outcome). I was allowed to retain several hardback chairs. Left to read by the glare of a naked bulb, since you had made off with the Tiffany replica lamp; and to eat on mismatched plates, since you had made off with the only intact set.

Your attorney, on the way out the door, served me with a permanent restraining order (the temporary one had since expired). You did not say goodbye. You did not express regret. You did not offer a fond reminiscence on our five years of wedded life, not even a halfhearted *wish things could have turned out otherwise*. You did not acknowledge any fault for having run off with Amber, for breaking my heart, for requesting spousal support and a partition of my childhood home, to which you had asserted a dubious claim, no doubt as leverage. If I am not mistaken, you muttered *thank God that's over*, before climbing into the U-Haul and making off with half my worldly possessions.

Rubinowitz, Esq., said *now is the ideal time to go on vacation.*

"I appreciate the advice, counselor. Truly I do." But I could not see myself at a singles-only, all-inclusive resort, lounging poolside. I could not see myself taking Greg L. up on his offer to go deep-woods camping. I could not envision myself squirrel shooting or going to the dinner theater in Schenectady to watch the revival of *Annie Get Your Gun*. I could not see myself happily residing with Dennis R., who had written a moving, if cliché-ridden paean to my worthy attributes, apropos of explaining how he could *be my everything*, including giving me all the space I claimed to need.

"Well, take care of yourself." He patted me on the hand. "I'll let you know when I receive the final papers. Once they're signed and notarized, you'll be rid of the bum," he assured me. "You'll be able to get on with your life. You'll see."

It was too much to assimilate. The clack of the screen door, the echo of footsteps. *Gone*.

Cadillac (U-Haul). Mother (husband). Foresworn to love and cherish you, they all abandon you in the end. Disappear down the path, never to be heard from again.

37

I remember the aroma of chocolate chip cookies, wafting through the house. I'd be roused from my preoccupations, my book or specimen collection, to go into the kitchen and wait next to her as the cake rose in its mold or the cookies plumped. The heat wafting from the oven. The kitchen a place of warmth and security, unlike the rest of the house, which my father kept at 55 degrees, lest anyone become too comfortable.

"Sit down, Ophelia. You can have the first one." Mother let the cookies cool, then slid them onto a rack. The aroma of chocolate and butter filled the kitchen. A dash of nutmeg. An aroma I would associate with her, long after she left. The aroma of warmth and heartbreak, of comfort and impending doom.

We sat at the table together. The late afternoon sun through the window, the loon echoing through the valley, the wind singing through the chimes.

"I wish it could be like this forever, bunny." *I wish it could be like this forever.* It was what she said when she tucked me in at night, when I stumbled upon the Easter eggs she'd hidden in the garden, when we drove to Lac des Pins, our luggage strapped to the top of the vehicle.

"Me too," I said. Already sensing, without knowing why, exactly, that it was ephemera. A bittersweet pinch, a dash of zest.

38

The door clacks. You (she) disappear down the path, never to be heard from again.

It was not enough that you had broken your marriage vows. You had to divest me of my sofa, my breakfast table, my crockery. You had to empty the drawers and pillage the cabinets and lay claim to any and every household item, even the silver-plated candelabra.

I had no sofa to sleep or binge eat on. Only several uncomfortable, straight-back chairs on which it was impossible to slump or to achieve any approximation of comfort. There were scuff marks on the floor where my Oriental carpet had been cruelly ripped up. The china cabinet had been emptied of stemware and plates and the crystal punch bowl, our only wedding gift of note.

Left without an espresso/cappuccino maker, I had to make do with Sanka and a can of Reddi-wip. Viennese Pleasures a poor substitute to the Caribou blend I used to make in my premium Nespresso. I might have made waffles, but the waffle iron was gone, along with the anodized cookware and skillet and any vestige of myself qua wife, qua loving spouse, qua human being.

My life had been depopulated, my house stripped: there was nothing left, nothing that hadn't been pried apart, ransacked, or mined.

In the pantry, I happened upon one long-expired can of baked beans. The electric opener gone, I had to pry it open with a rusty manual one. I ate my dinner on a tray you had been kind enough to leave me with, having made off with the kitchen table. I had purchased a screw top vintage at the wine store, or I'd be faced with opening wine without the benefit of a corkscrew. You'd helped himself to that item as well.

Lacking stemware, I decided to swig directly from the bottle. A halfway respectable vintage from the Finger Lakes region. A place where we had also vacationed, looking for antiques and items to populate the house. The house in which I now sat, rigidly upright, watching the television (you had seen fit to leave the flat screen, lacking the patience to unbolt it from the wall).

I watched *Snapped.* Stories of jilted wives and cuckolded husbands, spouses who had taken the law into their own hands. The particulars were lurid and riveting. The girlfriends young and tawdry. The reenactments crude and poorly acted. *Hearing that her husband had taken up with his assistant, an ivory-complected twenty-two-year-old, Mary could no longer go on. She surprised them at the office one day, brandishing a pearl-handled .22. Her husband tried to disarm her, but the bullet went off...*

Ophelia was happily married to Andrew. She fell asleep in his arms every night, and every morning made him toast, charred ever so slightly and cut on the diagonal. She waved goodbye when he went on "business trips." Ever so trusting, ever so in love, she assumed that he was going on sales calls, attending medical conferences. When she attempted to reach him, receiving the message *the cellular subscriber you have called is currently unavailable,* she assumed that he was delivering a sales pitch, demonstrating proper guidewire insertion techniques, but never, *ever,* that he was fornicating with a colleague, fabricating expense reports, spending weekends at the Atlantis resort, frolicking in the waves.

The wife rents the next-door room at the Minnie Ha-Ha. She listens to the alarming sounds of their lovemaking. The crash of a table lamp, the rattling of the headboard as he pounds away. The unspeakable exclamations, *Amber, you're so hot, fuck me, baby.* Her heart beats out of her chest. She is unable to comprehend. She floats above herself, a shadow on the ceiling. She alerts the police to an unspecified disturbance.

The husband walks out. He packs a bag. He strips the house of anything of worth, having the audacity to take the juicer her sisters (albeit estranged, albeit only half-sisters) sent as a belated wedding present.

The wife watches the husband. She observes his comings-and-goings, recording same in leather-bound notebooks. The contemporaneous record of his adulterous affair, meticulously notated, with dates and times and supporting details. Yet no one seems to care. The divorce court is interested only in division of the marital res.

The husband has made it clear he wants nothing further to do with the wife. He never wants to see her again. He asks that the parties waive court appearances and be apprised of the entry of the final decree of divorce via mail.

The wife questions herself. Her sanity, her recollection of events. Did she imagine that they were happy, once upon a time? Did she imagine that he was a willing and engaged participant in the marriage? That he proposed one night on the porch to the sing-song of cicadas, the moon bright and fulsome? Did she imagine these things? The memories like grooves.

I love you, Ophelia. As it turns out, entirely in the conditional, in the aspirational form. The husband never loved the wife, not as she loved him.

39

You and Amber snuggled on the sofa. The sofa on which we had lain, entwined (or at least within touching distance) watching television. On which we ate bag upon bag of potato chips, forgoing meals as we settled in for a marathon of *Law & Order.* The sofa where you whispered in my ear, *I love you,* an unmistakable declaration of affection, even if you never displayed for me the same fervor you exhibited when chasing Amber round the sofa and throwing her over your shoulder and dragging her into the bedroom like a Neanderthal.

When I was a child, I would practice erasing things from memory. A process of reverse development. I would see a puppy, or a duckling, and wait for the image to dissolve. I would think of our vacation at Lac des Pins, imagine the warm sand and the rippling waves, and I would white it out from memory, as if it had never existed. I would imagine Mother at the table, fixing a peanut butter sandwich, and I would let the image fade, until I could no longer make out her features, until she was unrecognizable.

The prison psychiatrist speculates that after a long period of living in what she characterizes as a "fantasy world," a "delusional domestic tableau" in which you and I were still in love, still conjoined, till death do us part, etc., etc.—I had no choice but to confront reality. Your continued cohabitation with Amber. Your usurpation of the marital furnishings and of various and sundry wedding gifts. Your insistence on keeping me at a fifty-foot distance, no communication whatsoever.

Your feelings for me had evaporated. Our marriage had irretrievably broken down. Whatever affection you once had for me—if indeed you ever loved me, which I question given the alacrity with which you made off with Amber—had dissipated.

The patient's inclination is to shun reality, to tune it out, unpleasant static. The mind regards events as transpiring elsewhere, in another dimension. A place far, far away. Eventually, the mind can no longer tolerate these fictitious distinctions. Long suppressed realities, unpleasant facts, eventually surface, with more violence than if they had initially been acknowledged.

Having made off with my sofa, the happy couple no longer needed Amber's horrid chintz one. Amber placed an ad on Craigslist. *Chintz couch, good condition, hardly used* (Oh, to what depraved uses it had been put, dear potential buyer! Do not gaze too closely upon the blooming rose, left arm rest.) *Make me an offer*, she glibly propositioned. I contacted Amber through Craigslist and made an appointment to see the sofa.

Can you describe the sofa more specifically? I asked, posing as Crazyforchintz.

Seven feet, matching footstool.

Can you upload more photographs?

Amber complied, sending back and front views.

Amber maintained that the posting had generated a lot of interest, insinuating that buyers were lining up to purchase the used, floridly upholstered couch. *Better get here soon, before it sells itself.*

I may or may not have tinkered with Amber's Craigslist account, diverting certain tepid responses and halfhearted inquiries (*not sure if it's for me, maybe it's worth a look????*), sorting out a weirdo or two (*Call me if you need to unload the sofa, I'm amiable, wink*), deflecting requests to view the item until midweek, after our rendezvous.

Amber had moved the couch into the garage, presumably to avoid the prospect of strangers trampling through her home, of would-be thieves informally assessing her worldly goods. I showed up at the appointed hour, introduced myself as Patty, a.k.a. Crazyforchintz.

I wore a blond wig and oversized glasses. I professed to own a tiny housewares shop in a small upstate hamlet (unspecified).

I was always on the lookout for a good quality item. I smiled too much and asked if I could have a cup of tea, if it was not too much trouble?

"It's no trouble," Amber reassured me. "Why don't you try it out? See if you like it."

While Amber rustled up a Lipton's tea bag from the kitchen, I looked around the garage. Boxes of your belongings stacked floor to ceiling (Andy, kitchen one, Andy, kitchen two). Boxes of medical supplies (samples, not for resale). Lulu's disassembled feeder. Her pink rhinestone collar. Leftover wee-wee pads (alas, she had never successfully been housebroken.)

The sight of the dead pet's belongings unnerved me. I felt a pang, a soupçon of remorse, for having unceremoniously clobbered her, for burying her under shallow fill in the neighboring yard. She at least deserved a decent burial, a fitting marker of her short span on earth, *beloved pet, rest in peace.*

I had not yet composed myself when Amber returned with my cup of tea.

"Are you okay?" she asked.

"Yes, quite," I recovered. "I was just looking at the dog collar. It reminds me of my long-lost pet."

My confession, however false, and motivated by a desire to avoid detection, moved Amber. "Me too," she whimpered. "My dog ran off and hasn't come home. I've looked all over the neighborhood, but no one's seen her." Amber shook her head. "I don't understand how she could just disappear. I miss her so much! They're really like family, you know?" She fell to sobbing.

I felt guilty for engendering this false camaraderie, for purporting to share her sorrow when I, in fact, had been the deviant engineer of the pet's demise. For depriving her of the proof, in whatever pecked-over and disturbing form, that her beloved pet was dead. Until such time, she would live in a state of willful disbelief, not knowing whether, at any given moment, Lulu would return, or whether she was gone forever. A feeling to which I could all too well relate, having watched my mother disappear down the garden path, never again to return.

I stumbled around the couch, purporting to examine it from every angle. I said I liked the lively print and bright colors.

I had gone with the intent of sizing her up, of rendering judgment. To evaluate her from a more objective perspective, rather than the limited one of a high-magnification viewfinder. To see her in the flesh, in three dimensions, rather than refracted through two-dimensional space that made certain objects appear closer than they actually were. To confirm that I was transcribing the proceedings of your relationship with fidelity, that certain linguistic patterns and lip movements were indeed as I had noted, that I had not mistaken *fuck you* for *I love you*, that I was not guilty of other interpretive biases.

It was my intent to engage in protracted negotiations over the item. To make a counter offer, and a counter-counter offer, to winnow the competition through selective deletion of items in her inbox, to force her to bargain with me, and only me, to either accept my lowball offer, or to leave it.

But I could not bring myself to engage in chitchat, to mumble anything more than *thank you for the tea, it's quite refreshing.* The sight of the poor animal's leash, and its glinting rhinestone collar, had unnerved me entirely.

The adulterer ranks low in Dante's hierarchy. Her offense is one of ungovernable emotion. Her *contrapasso*, in Dante's schema, is separation from the earthly body, the instrument of sin. She can no longer embrace the beloved, but is forced to watch him as they float, in eternity, incorporeal.

The pet murderer finds no sympathy. The victim is frequently furry and cute, with sad, liquid eyes. The victim wags its tail and jumps for a pet treat. Whosoever harms an innocent household pet cannot be right in the head. Whosoever harms a pet is on the road to perdition, whether or not she has technically violated the penal code of the State of New York.

I mumbled something about needing to think it over, and ran out. I heard the crash of the teacup as I hastened down the driveway and jumped into the car.

The world receding in the rearview. The road ahead narrowing. The juncture between Route 25 and the highway. A right path and a wrong path. The way of virtue. The way of vice.

Ladies and gentlemen, I submit to you that the defendant knew exactly what she was doing when, posing as Crazyforchintz, she contacted Amber and arranged to inspect the couch. The defendant wanted to see if Amber recognized her. She needed to ensure that she had a means of gaining access to the house. She had a pretext—couch for sale. She taped over the lock on the door leading from garage to house, ensuring that she could enter and exit the house at will. She knew exactly what she was doing...

Amber texted *have u made up ur mind? no pressure*, with a happy face emoji, presumably indicating that she thought the couch and me would make a good match, what with my sunroom and festive color palette.

I did not respond. I allowed her to think that I'd found another chintz more to my liking, or that I'd found a defect in the item—a busted spring, a tear in the fabric. Eventually I replied, *sorry have to pass.* I did not conclude with a ☺ to mitigate the affront, but let the words speak for themselves.

Amber said she understood and thanked me for my interest (sad-faced emoji). She responded to other inquiries about the couch (now that I was no longer rerouting them through a phony email account and a server in a remote Chinese province). She dutifully uploaded photos and replied promptly to questions regarding wear and tear and the condition of the springs. She engendered such good feelings that she was rated a five-star seller, not a single complaint. She earned effusive compliments (*Responds quickly and pleasantly—a pleasure to do business with her!*) People like Amber do not allow adversity to overwhelm them. They do not take rejection personally. They fervently believe in themselves. No one will ruin their day, let alone negatively affect the entirety of their lives, trauma emanating outward in deepening, concentric rings. No one will cause them to think a single negative thought about themselves, let alone to construct entire fallacious belief systems concerning their self-worth and value as human beings.

Amber sold the couch to Hotwheels45, across town. He arrived with a small U-Haul and a friend to cart it off. *Sur le champs*, he was persuaded to buy Amber's bookcase (Who needed books? They were doing her a favor!).

40

I decided not to contest the divorce. I agreed to dispense with formalities like strict compliance with Article 10 *et seq.* of the Domestic Relations Law, which required that I be personally served with any final decree of divorce; and to allow entry of reciprocal orders of protection, ensuring that we remained in our separate spheres, legally prohibited from coming within a twenty foot radius of one another (my attorney advised me to consent, lest unpleasant allegations regarding alleged eavesdropping and interception of electronic surveillance resurface, leading to unwanted referrals to the federal authorities).

Now that you and Amber were under no legal impediments to marriage, now that you were free to check into the Minnie Ha-Ha under your legal names, now that you were unshackled, liberated, free to do as you pleased, how long before you became bored? Before you'd had enough of her obvious charms? Before you could no longer look upon her countenance? Before you were tired of her too-perky breasts and teased updo, before you longed for someone, anyone else?

I waited. And waited. For affection to wane, for desire to shrivel. For love, once so ardent, to curdle.

I chanced to bump into Madge Loomis in the faculty office. She was teaching a summer course on remedial writing for incoming freshman we had perhaps too rashly admitted, overexuberant about their talents and future prospects. She had to educate them regarding finer points of grammar (hint: the plural form takes an added "s"; apostrophes are for possessives), inculcate an appreciation of the parts of speech (a noun is a person, place, or thing), aiming for at least a primitive level of expression, skills that might at least permit them to muddle through an unchallenging essay exam.

"Ophelia!" she exclaimed. I'd never understood why she seemed so happy to see me, when my closest relations had shunned me, balked from contact. "I've been thinking about you." She made an exaggerated frown, indicating her concern with my well-being.

"How are you, Madge?" I managed a twitching smile. Lack of Vitamin D, among other deficiencies, had led to facial spasming.

"You look so pale, hon! You need to get some sun. Go to Lac des Pins for the weekend," she suggested, mentioning the site of our last family vacation, the scene of unfortunate drowning—even the omen of a child dragged near lifeless from the waters, gasping for breath, insufficient to cause my mother to revise her plans, to decide against running off with Bob, used Cadillac salesman.

"I'm not one for sunbathing," I replied, citing my naturally pale complexion and tendency to overheat.

"Let's do something!" she insisted. Her beau was out of town (a job fair in Buffalo), and she was a *free woman*, able to stumble in at five o'clock in the morning without having to endure interrogation. Free to exchange telephone numbers with whomever she felt mildly attracted to (or at least not terribly repelled by), thereafter to delete them from memory.

"I don't mean to be insensitive." On the cusp of divorce from a philanderer, I was, understandably, sensitive to the topic of cheating. On the other hand, what did Madge owe Richie, to whom she was not legally tethered; who, albeit a domestic partner entitled to health insurance under our university's generous policies, had never pledged himself to her, or bought a ring, not even a microscopic chip from Zales.

"Is the divorce final?" Madge whispered, looking around.

"It will be in sixty days," I replied. The statutorily imposed waiting period before a marriage could be torn asunder, before the sanctified contract could be nullified, before the parties could go on their merry way, remarrying whomsoever they chose.

"So sorry." Madge shook her said. "It's all so distressing," she commiserated. "I guess you can never really know someone," she said, parroting the tag line of *Snapped.*

"More than you can imagine," I sighed. I felt the need, uncharacteristically, to unburden myself. To share my misery, to seek comfort in another, even if all she could do was nod and shake her head and murmur *asshole* as I recounted the story of your sordid affair with Amber. How I happened upon you shacked up at the Minnie Ha-Ha (omitting any mention of how I had followed you there; insinuating that I had merely been in the neighborhood). How I uncovered your trove of love letters in a drawer (a figurative drawer, a locked file), describing in graphic detail how much *you loved to fuck her brains out* (the implication, obviously, that you were presently with someone withholding, uptight, and possibly frigid; in any event, averse to watching herself make love in a mirror). How you had the nerve—although living with Amber, in a fully-furnished bungalow—to lay claim to the bulk of the household furnishings and the anodized cookware, leaving me with one pitiable crockpot. Etcetera, etcetera.

"Oh, honey!" she exclaimed. "You poor thing." She shook her head. "You've really been through the wringer."

Memories heavily revised so as to downplay the disturbing particulars. Events wrung of emotion, too difficult to contemplate or to fathom.

A sob surfaced, from where I knew not. Followed by lachrymose secretions, viz., tears, streaking down my face. I buried my face in my hands, not wanting to be seen, not wanting to be perceived as someone with feelings that could be trampled upon or savagely disregarded, though of course (as the prison psychiatrist noted, dumbfounded at the number of possible diagnoses, the manifold axes of dysfunction) I was a ravaged soul, irreparably wounded, beyond the help of traditional psychiatry.

"There, there. Let it all out," Madge encouraged me. I rested

my head on her shoulder, sniffled. "We're going out. It's decided. Get dressed up and I'll pick you up around seven. Wear
something nice." She winked.

I took a long, soaking bath. Exfoliated with a loofah.

I looked at myself in the full-length mirror. My hair, combed
into submission, looked attractive. My cheeks, hollowed out
from the weight loss, looked chiseled.

I espied a form-fitting dress from the closet. A miracle fabric
(10 percent nylon, 90 percent Lycra) that minimized bulges and
provided strategic uplift. I was not accustomed to drawing attention to myself, to thrusting myself out there, shoving breasts
together and upward, where anyone might gaze upon them. I
was not used to flaunting my physical attributes, to corseting
myself up and slipping into heels, shifting my point of gravity.
I had spent my life hiding, distancing myself from my physical form, dissociating myself from my physical surroundings,
a process of unbecoming, hoping thereby to erase the disturbing
particulars of my life.

It was time to get out there. To be the object of attention,
rather than the observer, the recorder, the obsessional diarist
and deranged voyeur, affixed to the viewfinder of the telescope.

I shimmied into the dress. I slipped into a pair of four-inch-
high stilettos. I opened a new set of Egyptian cotton sheets,
four hundred thread count; I scented the air with exotic fra-
grance (Jasmine? A patchouli blend from the hardware store?).
The night was young, the midsummer air balmy. The moon
three-quarters full.

Madge made a reservation at Uptempo, an upscale jazz bistro.
No danger of running into Zeke or Rob. No chance of a skir-
mish with Darlene, the fortyish waif in cut-off denims who
had never, apparently, worn a bra (*don't like 'em, too stifling*, she
opined, while swigging a bottle of tequila). No hanky-panky in
the bathroom, contorting over rust-stained fixtures.

A chanteuse in a red sequined dress (*We are proud to welcome*

Odette Markham, frequent performer at the Marriott chain!) took the
stage.

We sat at the bar, eating rock shrimp and sipping tepid Pe-
ruvian chardonnay. I in my miracle fiber dress, Madge in a low-
cut silk blouse and miniskirt. My breasts popping out, Madge's
barely tethered together by her bra. My body *ahum* with the
Brazilian bossa nova.

Perhaps because we looked fetching, perhaps because it was
ladies' night (ladies drink free!), we found ourselves the recip-
ients of many a complimentary glass. Madge was slurring her
words before we even properly made the acquaintance of Todd
and his friend Charlie, in town for a convention of insurance
agents.

"Nice to meet you, ladies." We clinked glasses. The chanteuse scatted, *da-doodily-bap-zee-BOP.*

Madge, via nonverbal cues (an exaggerated wink, a surreptitious kick under the table), let it be known that of the two she
preferred Charlie. They proceeded to grope one another on the
banquette, ignoring us entirely.

Left alone with Todd, I was forced to interact, to carry on
a conversation, to engage in chitchat. To nod my head, to in-
terject on occasion (appropriate mirroring behavior). To flirt
(arm stroking arm, leg grazing leg). To hold his gaze (nonverbal
behavior indicating openness, lack of anything to hide).

I could play the role of the seductress. Place an olive on his
tongue and suggest (as he swallowed my fingers whole, lick-
ing between them) that we go back to his hotel room. Discard
my clothing—my Lycra-blend dress, my uplifting bra—as he
watched, trying to catch a glimpse of us in the mirror. Beckon-
ing him, yanking playfully on his tie, reeling him in. The shadows throw various aspects into relief, concealing others.

He likes to talk when he is making love, to establish a human
connection. *I find you so attractive,* he whispers in my ear. He likes
to narrate what he is doing. *I am going inside you now. Do you prefer
it this way?* I watch us wrestle on the bed, tangled in one another,
filling the empty spaces. The ceiling fan creaks; Nina Simone is

playing somewhere, off in the distance. I watch us kiss. He pulls me closer, grasping my buttocks, shuddering into my chest, but I am floating above, on another plane, a dispassionate observer.

In the whole of my life, I have only allowed one to inhabit my interior spaces, to see me qua me. I have only allowed one to see me as I am, unreflected, unposed, unadjusted, *as is*. Only one to dwell within my heart, to fill the void left by Mother. The devastating clack. The reverberating steps. The lingering *fermata*.

You.

I stumbled out of bed, murmured apologies for having *to have fun and run*, scribbled my number on hotel stationery (*Call me*, followed by the number of the local animal shelter), and dashed out the door.

41

L ife makes its impression on each of us in different ways. There are those of us who escape with nary a mark. There are others who are caught in riptides and smashed against the pilings. We are compelled to reenact certain psychodramas. The mother-abandoner. The father-morbid depressive. She left, the screen door clacking behind her, never to be seen or heard from again; he remained, but withdrew, purporting to be there, though not there, his mind consumed with other matters, an abdication of his role qua father. Hers an act of (omission). His, a bloody mess, an inevitable trajectory.

Events subject to (fruitless) speculation. No amount of role-playing, of arguing on her behalf, of assuming her point of view, of taking out my frustrations on therapeutic pillows, imparts understanding.

Memories like grooves.

I led Madge to believe that Todd and I had hit it off. When interrogated regarding the events of the night in question, I winked and let it be inferred that relations had been magical, gravity-defying. I confirmed that we had exchanged working telephone numbers, valid email addresses. That we had made plans, tentatively, to see each other the following weekend.

"I'm so proud of you for getting out there!" Madge exclaimed. "You see! I knew you'd get over your ex, eventually. It just takes time."

"He said he could see himself falling for me." I blushed.

"That's fantastic, hon!" Madge squealed.

"He's, uh, divorced too. No children."

"You see! He understands."

I neglected to mention the fact that I had given Todd a false telephone number, that aside from my name, he knew nothing about me. Nothing of my past, of the serial abandonments. *A fortiori*, nothing regarding my nighttime activities, my watch from the abandoned and foreclosed Lark property, my observations through the telescope. The unfortunate incident with Lulu. The improvised burial near the property line, deep enough to avoid scavengers (or so I thought).

We are angled away from one another, in positions only partially revealing. We conceal our faults, our imperfections, presenting only our best side. Reflections of false selves.

42

*A*mber *packing. Stuffs five(!) valises with neon swimwear and flouncy negligées. Après-soleil tanning products. Enough lubricant for a whorehouse.*

She twirls around the house, mouthing the words to "Pour Some Sugar on Me." Def Leppard, vintage 1987. She does not pack any reading material. Not even a bodice ripper, or one of the young adult novels of which she is fond, apparently never having aged out of the category. There are faint, shimmery lines near her buttocks. I have seen them from various angles. An exaggeration, perhaps, to call them stretch marks. But undoubtedly an imperfection, visible in a certain light.

I watch her dance around. So agile, able to pop into a split and bounce back up. Back in her cheerleading days at Akron High, she topped pyramids and cartwheeled in short skirt and lace-frilled panties.

She locks herself in the bathroom. Her body distorted by the pebbled glass—a medium meant to deter crazed voyeurs, erotic intermeddlers, those seeking to eavesdrop on intimate moments.

She inspects herself in the magnifying mirror. Ensures that no stray hairs mar her perfect brow line. Pluck, PLUCK. She scrubs her skin with a cleansing mask from Provence, a gommage (I squint) of shea butter, evening primrose seeds, and xanthan gum. Applies moisturizer about the elbows and knees, desiccated regions in even the most vigilant moisturizers among us. Scrunches up her hair, spritzing, giving me ideas for how to volumize. Daubs concealer under her eyes, minimizing under-eye circles. She applies gloss, blots, then finishes with two coats of lipstick. She outlines first, then fills in the contours.

According to Amber's Facebook page, you were en route to the Cayman Islands. A beachside villa, steeply discounted owing to hurricane season. Starry nights, palm trees, the insufferable humidity that is the Caribbean in late summer.

43

While you frolicked in the saltwater pool, and paid $350 to stroke the skins of dolphins—preternaturally sensitive creatures they, and so delightful, with their arcing leaps and click-click-clicks! —I took up residence in the bungalow.

I dozed on and off while enjoying a *Hoarders* marathon. Sprawled out on the sofa—my sofa—munching on artisanal potato chips I found in the cupboards.

I lounged on the sofa, spilling crumbs on the floor, allowing beer oops!—to foam over, staining the carpet

I slept in your bed. I drooled on your pillow, leaving the im print of my body on your memory foam. When next you made love to Amber, tackled her on the bed, and tore off her panties with your teeth, the mark of me would remain. A frazzled hair, a fingernail clipping.

I took a bath in your tub, using Amber's exfoliating body paste and body wash from the Loire Valley. I scrubbed my scalp with gentle cleansing shampoo. I rinsed and wrapped myself in Amber's bathrobe. I may have rummaged in her underwear drawer, turning over her bras. We shared a bra size, if little else. Whereas hers were perky, gravity-defying, mine, alas, were in need of considerable support. The T-shirt bras of which she was fond—lacking the structural support, the undergirding of more traditional brassieres—were for me unworkable.

I brushed my hair with one of her brushes (leaving a brown interloper among the frosted blond strands) and padded around in her comfortable slippers (I suffered from foot fungus—oops—a communicable malady). I made a copy of the house keys (they were hanging—hanging!—from a hook in the kitchen), enabling me to slip in and out without jimmying the lock or taping it over or squeezing through half-shut windows.

What Amber had stolen from me, I would steal from her. Quid pro quo. I would inhabit her house, eat on her plates, sprinkle my crumbs about the house, heedless of wherever they fell. I would lather myself in her tub and vigorously dry using her linens. I would sleep on her half of the bed, making an indelible mark on the memory foam. I would wear her bras and her track suits, seeing what it was like to inhabit her skin, to wear lurid colors, to be the vixen. To be the one you chose.

44

I have been asked many times, during the course of this ordeal, to give an account of the events leading up to the crimes. I have been subjected to lengthy interrogation at the Saratoga County police station, only a package of Twizzlers and a four-ounce cup of water to sustain me. Made to go over the pertinent facts, to exhume every detail, no matter how seemingly trivial or insignificant. I have been asked to sign sworn statements waiving my rights, to confirm my understanding that anything said could be used against me in a court of law (exhausted nod, scribbled signature). To decipher the cramped and sometimes unintelligible writing in Observations I through VII (the notebooks had been discovered by an enterprising detective underneath the floorboards in the abandoned Lark property, during a last sweep before the house was consigned to dust by the bulldozers).

What others might view as depraved indifference to human life may instead be understood as the remnants of a traumatic childhood. A callous façade adopted for purposes of survival, not the manifestations of an "evil and malevolent intelligence," as the prosecutor asserted in summation.

I submit to you that Miss Amber Halloway was not an innocent, but a cunning vixen, intent on smashing the sacred marital bond. She seduced the husband, co-opting his affections; she enticed him, three times per week, at the Minnie Ha-Ha, their sordid love nest off the post road. She encouraged him to find fault with the wife—wife pain in ur ass, wife loco, wife doesn't deserve u, u are too cute!—the wife who had loved and supported him through dry spells and cadaver shortages. She encouraged him to abandon the wife, to take up residence in her cozy bungalow, where they might fornicate free of interference and long-distance nagging (Where are you? Why aren't you home?). She pranced around the bungalow in obscene underwear, in sheer bras and panties that left little to the imagination and attested to the vigorousness of her waxing routine. She encouraged him to file for divorce, to shatter the sacred bond with the wife, till death do us part, etc., giving little care to what havoc she was wreaking, what long-standing grievances and traumas she was awakening, the long shadows of abandonment and the insecurities attendant to the shotgun death of the father (barrel in mouth, aiming upward and through the pons: death a certainty). A homewrecker, like Bob before her, indifferent to the ramifications of her actions, indifferent to the fall-out: rages for which no foam pillow is ever adequate.

45

I divined, from Facebook postings (Vacation of a lifetime! Sunset walks! The dolphins are *so cute*) that you and Amber were returning on the eleventh of August. I circled the date on the wall calendar.

The sinner, as he passes from this life to the one beyond, has one last chance to acknowledge his sins. To admit what he has done wrong, to ask for forgiveness. (The Christian tradition allows for one last reprieve. Other religions are not so generous. A life of perfidy cannot be salvaged by a last, desperate act of contrition.)

Puttering about the house, watering the ficus, I attracted the attention of the neighbor across the way. Mallory rang the bell, demanding to know my credentials. I purported to be Amber's childhood friend from Akron. I introduced myself as *Patty*, the name of my chintz buying doppelgänger. I feigned exuberance for the happy couple, whom I described as *made for one another* and *so much in love*. I made her a double cappuccino with half and half—the machine, after all, had been mine until fairly recently.

"Amber's been so much happier since she met Andy," Mallory enthused.

"Yes," I said. The cup—once part of a matched set—trembled in my hands.

"She really deserves it," mused Mallory. "After Greg." Mallory rolled her eyes. "He was a piece of work."

"I know." I stirred the sugar until it thoroughly dissolved. "None of us liked him."

"Who would?" Mallory shook her head, availing herself of the shortbread cookies I had set out on a plate, not wanting to seem unwelcoming. "He really put her through the wringer. Well, that's thankfully in the past. Amber deserves to be happy.

She has such a big heart. So much to give. She and Andy are so cute together!"

I tried to suppress the gestures said to betray our true emotions. The sneer. The knuckles cracking. First metacarpal, second metacarpal, *rip*.

"You must be so happy for her! After everything she's been through. Poor thing. She's a trooper. Never gave up hope."

"Uh-huh." I nodded vigorously. "Forgive me, but I understood Andy to be only recently separated. To be in the process of a divorce."

"Oh, wait a minute," said Mallory, upon reflection. "She did mention that he'd been married. To someone older. But they'd fallen out of love."

"Excuse me?" I sputtered.

"Well, as described to me, it seemed more like a marriage of convenience. Not a love match. She was a bit strange. A college professor," Mallory tssked.

"Is there something wrong with being a college professor?" I inquired, hand trembling, cup tittering on the saucer.

"I just mean that she was a little off-putting. A depressive too. She'd go off on her own for hours on end. Brooding about this or that. Not a good communicator. Not good about expressing her feelings."

"I see," I said, jaw tight, temples throbbing. Why is it a virtue to confide in others, to blather about feelings, to implicate others in our tragedies? I was just being considerate.

"I just know what I've been told. Third-hand gossip," she laughed. "Amber described her as blahh. Not unattractive, but kind of plain."

Who among us could compete with the glowing and preternaturally fit Ms. Halloway? Who could fit into a size 2, even on our best day? Certainly not I. I gulped the tea, scalding my tongue.

"Are you all right?" Mallory shrieked.

I tried desperately to maintain my grip on the cup. To stop

the unwitting clattering. To avoid the splatter as the hot liquid spilled forth and onto the kitchen table.

Alas, I was not all right, dear Mallory, but trying to maintain a desperate semblance of *all right*, a simulacrum of a normal, psychologically whole human being. One capable of tea party conversation; one who could brush off commentary about her *strange and brooding nature*, stop internalizing, allowing others' assessments to erode her precarious self-esteem.

I sopped up the spilt liquid and offered Mallory a conciliatory macchiato with chocolate shavings. "It's no bother, really," I persisted. I had mastered the owner's manual. I knew a latte from a latte macchiato! I knew just the right amount of pressure to apply in order to brew a Caffè Americano!

"That's okay." Mallory waved her hand. "I have to get going. There's a garden show downtown! I'm trying to get a head start on the begonias."

"Well, thanks for stopping by!" I chirped.

There are those who cry on the neighbor's shoulder, eliciting pity. Those who share their woes over white wine or margaritas, seeking affirmation for their suffering, *poor you, things will get better, just you see!* Others whose wounds are too deep to fathom. The dimensions of their pain can only be guessed at. They see no point, no constructive one, in recounting their serial traumas. They find no comfort in describing the particulars of their woe. Merely touching upon their sad circumstances threatens to awaken buried feelings, to start an avalanche of repressed emotion.

46

Through an outfit catering to the penitentiary population (*Remember to include your prison ID number!*, the order form chastised), I ordered the following titles: *How to Make Sailors' Knots*, *Common Poisonous Household Plants*, and *Ninja Death Touch*. How-to advice for making unslippable knots and inducing temporary unconsciousness via selective pressure to the carotid *(Just don't press too hard!)*. Caveat: for informational purposes only. The books arrived in plain brown wrapping, the return address obscured. *Just sign here* [scribble].

I drove to the Home Depot in Schenectady, thirty miles away, to purchase miscellaneous household items. Wandered up and down the aisles, weighing the efficacy of zip ties against rope, evaluating the force per square inch afforded by the fire safety ax, taking note of the weekly special *(three rolls of duct tape for the price of one!)*. Jake, sales associate, rendered invaluable assistance, helping me ultimately decide in favor of The Dudgeon, a club designed to subdue meddlesome strays, mid-size wild animals, and escaped convicts on the loose.

"We recommend The Dudgeon for women on their own," he said, singletons having anxieties associated with living alone in an emptied house with creaking noises and disturbing memories. "It's easy to yield, gets the job done, multi-purpose." Effective in hacking out of burning buildings as well as subduing unruly husbands. "It's one of our bestselling items," he added.

"I'll need some duct tape too," I added, as he tallied up my purchases—rope, duct tape, a bludgeoning instrument. "Don't worry." I laughed, perhaps too readily, *it's not like I'm planning on taking hostages or anything*. "I want to thank you kindly for all of your assistance, uh, Jake," I said, hoping he would earn a handsome commission.

"What did you say your name was?" he inquired.

"Patty," I said, the name of my alter-ego, the one who shopped for chintz couches and befriended unknowing neighbors.

I avoided toll routes where my image might be captured on grainy surveillance footage. The summer air thick, choked with humidity. On the merge with I-90, I vied for the left lane with a minivan, eventually cutting them off. They would be advised to pay attention to the road instead of bantering, watching Disney franchise films on their DVD screens, daydreaming about Lake George, or Lake Oswego, or wherever they were going with their *I Honk for Canada Geese* bumper sticker and the canoe strapped on the roof of the car.

The heat rippled in waves. A mirage when one stares too long at the horizon, at the vanishing point where the earth drops off.

I stopped for gas at the Stop N Gulp off Exit 15, paying in cash. *Fill it up, please. And I'll take a package of the jerky.*

The sun sank lower. I contemplated the night, the darkening night. All that was visible and invisible, the after images of what once was. The abyss swallows us whole, allowing no light to escape. I considered the likelihood that I would reach home before midnight, having taken several detours and lost my way along the forested path.

Sitting disconsolately on the asphalt curb, gnawing on a piece of jerky, I attracted the attentions of an itinerant trucker who was transporting a load of timber south from Quebec. "Do you want to get a cup of coffee, hon?" he asked.

"You'll forgive me if I decline," I replied. Jean-Claude, in his diesel-stained shirt and foul-smelling breeches, would not be my guide to the underworld. What hurried and unsatisfactory intercourse had he engaged in, cramped in the cab of his tractor-trailer? What sad woman had he promised to look up on his next run through?

"It's you who'll regret it." He swaggered by, entered the convenience store, and exited with a six pack of malt liquor.

Perhaps I would, Jean-Claude. Perhaps I would regret this

last chance to commune with another soul, to tangle in the sheets, to purport to be in love, if only for the minute or two of thrusting it would take before he emptied himself inside me.

"Maybe I will," I said, inhaling deeply once he had passed, the whiff of him dissipating.

47

Harrowing, *adj.* Causing especial affright.
Harrow, *v.*, *transitive*, to visit the precincts of Hell.
Harrowing, *noun.* A descent through the underworld.

My mother having failed to return for a month, six months, a year, I finally broke my silence. "When is she coming back, Daddy?" I asked, an inquiry that was met with a resounding slap.

I strove, thereafter, not to press my father for information, not to ask direct questions, disturbing him as little as possible. Mere mention of her name, no matter how innocently, resulted in swift caning and calumnies along the lines of *I wish you'd never been born. How am I supposed to take care of a child now?* He re mained alone, biding time, ensuring that I had reached the age of majority before sticking a shotgun into his mouth. Through the roof of the mouth, into the pons, explosion of brain matter: death instantaneous.

Abandon hope, all ye who enter here.

By the time I reached home, it was after midnight. I tried to squeeze the Volvo into Amber's garage. Knocked over a garbage can. Gored several cardboard boxes in my attempt to correct the steering.

The commotion roused Mallory from sleep. A light went on in the slumbering Cape Cod. The blinds opened. Mallory, nose pressed against the glass, *What's going on?*

I had already aroused suspicions by my sudden appearance at the bungalow. Suspicions I had gone through great lengths to allay—befriending the intrusive Mallory, making her double lattes, setting her at ease with entirely fictive narratives concerning my relationship to Amber and my reasons for passing through bucolic upstate New York. I was wary of jeopardizing whatever rapport we had established. I was fearful of squandering whatever trust I had earned during our lengthy chat sessions. We were both of us fans of *Hoarders*, conversant with the obsessions that had driven Evangeline S. to make Tupperware shrines to her departed loved ones. Both of us were distressed that Floyd C., despite severe asthma and chronic pulmonary disease, continued to live among moldering cartons and roach-festooned takeout containers. I did not want to alienate Mallory—not when so much work lay ahead. Mastery of the double hitch; practice wielding The Dudgeon; overcoming whatever mental reservations I still had about bludgeoning culpable parties or exacting justice for their transgressions.

And now she was staring at me, face distorted by the window glass. The observed watching the observer, the two locked in an uncomfortable gaze.

I mouthed the word *sorry*, also the word *lost*.

She nodded. Turned off the high-wattage bulb and returned to bed.

For the time being, she was satisfied with my explanation. Willing to suspend disbelief, to refrain from calling the police. To look away as I unpacked the trunk, removing duct tape and zip ties therefrom.

From after images and scattershot reflections, we make our own truths. From flimsy evidence and biased accounts, we construct our own narratives.

Ladies and gentlemen of the jury, I submit to you that the defendant laid a trap for her husband and Ms. Halloway, a clever and diabolical trap. She procured items from the Home Depot in Schenectady, over thirty miles away, using cash. She drove back routes so as to escape detection. On one occasion, stopping by to leave a letter that had mistakenly been placed in her mailbox, the neighbor saw the defendant practicing knots, exploding in anger when she was unable to make the double hitch, a knot prominently circled in How to Make Sailors' Knots, *a book procured by the defendant and heavily marked up, with disturbing marginalia.*

My concentration, my ability to focus on the task at hand, was compromised by the meddling interventions of Mallory. No sooner had I curled up with *How to Make Sailors' Knots*, than she was at the door, claiming to be out of sugar, or mayonnaise, or some other condiment. No sooner had I retired to the couch with my laptop, refamiliarizing myself with your itinerary, tracking tropical storm Lucy, torturing myself with photo galleries of you swimming with the dolphins, than she was on the doorstep, returning a misdelivered letter, asking me if I hadn't received her correspondence from Publishers Clearing House, or the latest issue of *Us Weekly*, the gossip rag from which she gleaned most of her information concerning reality television stars and washed-up screen icons, a veritable catalog of has-beens and never-beens, and almost-weres, had they the forethought not to appear in *Saw X*, or the strength to resist the producer intent on signing a Grade V hoarder.

"I'm sorry, Mallory, I haven't received any of your correspondence."

My denials, my unequivocal refutations, my pleas of being otherwise engaged, did not prevent Mallory from inviting herself in, from looking around, from opening and shutting the cupboards, from wandering down the long hallway and into the bathroom and rummaging in the medicine cabinets.

"Overactive bladder," she maintained, by way of explanation.

I was growing tired of the flimsy excuses. The urgent need to reclaim a flour sifter she had lent Amber the month previous. The sudden desire for a cappuccino with nutmeg shavings. The impromptu suggestion that we watch the *Hoarders* marathon together.

With Mallory underfoot, I had limited time to devote to *How to Master Sailors' Knots*, less to devote to mastery of the silent sleeper chokehold (from another charming book, this one entitled *Ninja Death Touch*), still less to full-scale dress rehearsal (I had to remove anything from the victims' purview that might be turned on me and used as a weapon, including the crystal decanters and the universal remote).

I missed the solitude to which I had become accustomed during my time on the Lark property. The basement space had allowed for contemplation, reflection, and of course obsessive rumination.

"Why don't we send Amber an email, let her know how well we're getting along! Tell her not to rush back," Mallory proposed one evening, as I tried, futilely, to dissuade her from watching an episode of *Snapped* with me.

"I don't think that's a good idea," I replied.

"Why not?"

"Well," I stalled, never particularly good at thinking on my feet, "she has reason to believe Andy is going to propose to her on the trip."

I shoveled ridged sour cream chips into my mouth. CRUNCH. A nervous habit of mine when confronted with unpleasantries I'd rather repress. An obsessive tendency, one among many, for coping with negative emotions and my lack of control over events transpiring around me.

"Oh my gosh! How exciting! They're such a lovely couple! So much in love!"

"Yes…" I trailed off. "I think it's best to let them be," I advised.

She seemed to accept this line of reasoning. My pleas for your privacy. My insistence that any pings or messages would be unwelcome. My promises to convey her congratulations promptly upon your return.

I set up a fake wedding registry for purposes of diverting her, sending her on an errand to procure a discontinued pattern that was temporarily out of stock. I encouraged her to go to the Fortunoff's in Danbury, Connecticut, where, as an out-of-state purchaser, she would be exempt from the onerous sales tax.

"Lenox no longer makes Asiatic pheasant blue," Mallory informed me. "I think we should let them know so they can pick another pattern."

How would I keep her occupied during our critical tête-a-tête? I could not risk her intruding just when I was making headway in the effort to convince you to renounce Amber and return home.

Eventually, I arrived at the conclusion that it would be best to drug Mallory for the duration of the confrontation. I had two 5 mg. capsules of Somnambulis remaining. It was enough to induce a pleasant torpor without the risk of habit-forming addiction or respiratory compromise. I would be certain to tell Mallory, when she reported an *overwhelming fatigue*, to suspend her search for the missing items on the wedding registry and to spend the day on the couch catching up on the episodes of *Hoarders* she had missed. Not to operate a moving vehicle, lest she crash into a tree, or drive the wrong way down a road.

The day of reckoning was fast approaching. The day when the observer would write herself into the scene, *becoming*, rather than engaging in passive observation, rote recording of events. The day when the observed, heretofore under the impression that his actions went unnoticed, would be called to account, to answer for his transgressions

Your return was delayed several days by the passage of tropical storm Lucy. I studied the swirling, color-coded weather maps disseminated by the National Weather Service, indicating landfall on the windward side of the island at 8:00 EST, winds approaching 75 miles per hour.

Nothing to do but wait.

Mallory and I spent the evening watching reruns of *Hoarders*. I had grown fond of her, notwithstanding the intrusions, the one-upmanship about A&E programming trivia (she had seen every episode of *Hoarders* at least twice, remembering who had a soft spot for Hummels, who slept in a trailer, who resisted all efforts at aftercare, repopulating her empty house with even more junk).

I'd never had a sibling (if one discounts the imposters from Florida who surfaced many years later, trying to capitalize on my organs). Someone whose companionship could mitigate the sense of terrible loss; someone who knew exactly what I had gone through, having suffered through it herself and perhaps having developed a more sanguine perspective.

I felt an affinity for Mallory, a bond that transcended our shared affinity for *Hoarders* and caramel macchiatos. The solidarity of two lost and lonely souls, those who had been deprived of human company for various and sundry reasons.

I considered for an instant, a fleeting instant, whether to confide in her, to reveal that I was not in actuality Patty from Akron, but rather, the elusive character known as Mrs. Andy Fairweather, soon to be the ex-Mrs. Andy Fairweather. To recount my distress at having discovered you to be involved with Amber—the assignations at the Minnie Ha-Ha, the rendezvous at the annual convention of medical device specialists, the strings of salivating and leering emojis appended to every communication.

But I could not risk it.

"Do you think she'll give up the dolls?" Mallory bit her fingers.

"If she's truly sincere about wanting to let go of the past," I said, echoing the words of Dr. Szaz, hoarding specialist.

Who among us wants to expire under an avalanche of board games and Cabbage Patch Kids? To draw her last breath under a crush of unsorted bric-a-brac? To be left unclaimed under a pile of Madame Alexander dolls? To be interred along with her Hello Kitty collectibles?

"She's not ready to give it up," Mallory observed. The process of sorting items was a nightmarish tug-of-war over sodden and moldering containers. *I won't give it up! You can't make me!* The 1-800-GOT-JUNK trucks idling at the curb.

It was eight o'clock. Twilight descending. I stared at the window, my reflection staring back at me. Our selves refracted unexpectedly in illuminating surfaces and paned glass. It was the opportune time for a test run. It was important to ascertain whether Mallory would drift into peaceful slumber when Somnambulis was stirred into her drink—*whisk!*—or whether she fell into the small but significant minority of users impervious to the drug's soporific effects. Whether she would experience any of the adverse effects reported in the packaging insert (WARNING: MAY LEAD TO RESPIRATORY COMPRO-MISE; IF YOU EXPERIENCE DIFFICULTY BREATH-ING DISCONTINUE IMMEDIATELY), or instead fall into a restorative, pleasing sleep. Whether I was capable of administering the unprescribed narcotic to Mallory—an unwitting bystander, a nettlesome neighbor—or whether my conscience would intervene.

"Would you like a Manhattan?" I asked.

I estimated the proper dosage—enough to make her sleepy, uninterested in the goings-on next door, but not so much as to depress respiration and endanger vital functions. I awaited the commercial interruption and slipped inside the kitchen. I endeavored to crush the pill using steady pressure. It was time-released to induce a pleasant state of drowsiness in the patient. To plunge her directly into a hypnagogic state, i.e., neither here nor there, suspended between this world and the one from which we might never awaken.

"Hurry, Patty! You'll miss the organizing specialist."

"Coming," I assured her. I mixed the soporific into her Man-hattan—thoroughly so as to dissolve the bitter granules.

"What's taking so long?"

"Nothing. I'll be right in." I was stricken with the impulse to call off the plan, to dump Mallory's cocktail down the drain, and to make her a Highball instead (we were running out of bitters). To pack up my belongings and return to the Victorian, where I could live out the rest of my days alone, renouncing any further designs on you and your charming fiancée.

"I hope you don't mind the cherry," I said. The glasses rattled as I entered the living room and set the tray down on the ottoman. The drinks seethed over the rim; the ice cubes foundered.

"Are you okay?" Mallory asked. I was touched by this concern for my well-being. Though we hadn't known each other long, I had grown fond of her. I had come to expect her nightly rap on the door, wondering whether I might not want to watch a program on the Arts & Entertainment channel, a refuge for so-called reality programs and reenactments of real-life crimes.

"I'm all right, Mallory. Just a little melancholy."

"I know how you feel." She patted my hand. And here she unburdened herself thoroughly, relating how her first husband had died in a car accident, how the second had succumbed to stomach cancer—leaving her a widow twice over, utterly alone.

The glass hovered at the entrance of her mouth. A first tentative sip.

"If you don't like it, I'll be happy to make you something else." I reached for the glass and almost upset its contents. "You don't have to pretend to like it. Why don't you let me make you something else—"

Playing devil's advocate. Pleading to be saved from my own reckless impulses.

"Don't be silly." She swatted my hand away. "I like it." She proceeded to down the contents of the glass, pausing only once. Murmuring something about *wow, what a kicker,* and *it tastes more bitter than I expected.*

I watched as the surprisingly fast-acting drug took effect. She was out within minutes. Verifiably unconscious (lifting arm, letting it drop back down, absolutely no resistance), unresponsive (pots clanged by her ear eliciting no response whatsoever), dozing in a netherworld.

Mallory! If only she hadn't stumbled into the middle of my devious plan, presented herself on the doorstep just as I was hunkering down for the final phase. If only she had been content to accept my initial explanation and left it at that, rather than pestering me for flour or sugar or whatever else was supposedly missing from her cupboard and needed urgent replacement.

I maintained vigil at her side, ensuring that she did not roll over, face down, and forget to breathe, the packaging insert having identified poor respiratory effort as a possible side effect. I monitored her vital signs, concerned that I might have miscalculated the dosage, overestimated the milligrams necessary to subdue Mallory, whose weight, hovering in the one hundred fifty to one hundred sixty range, was difficult to pinpoint. I looked for signs of an unknown drug sensitivity, of an unforeseeable and potentially fatal drug interaction (not having perused her medicine cabinet, I had no idea what medications she had been prescribed or in what dosages).

I remained awake, watching my charge, half-following the storyline of the season finale of *Hoarders*. Seemingly normal, middle-aged women, displaced by household possessions and the weight of their accumulated sorrows. When life becomes too much to bear, there is comfort in the certainty of a paper drink umbrella, in the knowledge that one possesses all eighteen iterations of the Magic Chef kitchen knife.

Mallory snored—an annoying habit that under the circumstances proved comforting, proof that she was alive and respiring. So long as there was a chance that she might not regain consciousness, a possibility that I had miscalculated the dosage, I had to remain awake, monitoring her vital signs. I watched as Dr. Szaz endeavored to convince an intractable hoarder to give up just one moldering plate, to identify one doll from among a collection of thousands that she could surrender without inducing a full-scale panic attack. The items were dragged onto the front lawn, where the hoarder was forced to wander among the piles of junk, *No, I want this; yes, I'll give up the cake plate*

Mallory awoke in the dead of night, gasping, complaining of dry mouth (one of the more common advertised side effects).

"Where am I?" she groaned, rubbing her eyes.

"Don't you remember?" I asked.

"Are we going to pick up the wine goblets?" she asked.

"Later." I patted her hand. "Right now, I think we should get you home." I helped her on with her sweater, shoving limp appendages into sleeves. I retrieved her shoes from under the sofa, where they had apparently been flung in the struggle to subdue her, and guided her across the street, one arm supportively around the shoulder, the other holding up her limp and heavy figure, looking both ways to ensure that no one saw me dragging her across the way in the dead of night. I gave her water to slake her thirst (warning: users may suffer from dry mouth and have difficulty swallowing) and put her to bed.

The following day, she had no recollection of the events of the night before. No memory of. confiding in me the sad circumstances surrounding the deaths of her first and second husbands; no recollection of coming over, let alone of imbibing a drugged Manhattan and passing out on the sofa.

She had only the strange sensation of time unaccounted for.

48

You were rerouted through Raleigh-Durham, where, along with approximately six hundred others who had been stranded during the storm, you were awaiting a return flight. In the meantime, you and Amber had been given temporary accommodation at the airport motel, a generous twelve-dollar meal voucher that you could spend at any one of the numerous area fast food establishments. How far you had fallen, from Caribbean over-the-water bungalow to the airport motel, where you were lucky to escape without bedbugs.

It gave me some solace to think that your escape had been marred by unforeseen circumstances; that the swirling, high-pressure clouds of tropical storm Lucy had interfered with your vacation, cutting into the time Amber could spend frolicking with the dolphins or working on her tan. Solace to think that you were sleeping in a motel room, taking your chances with the plastic ice bucket, afraid to touch any surface in the room for fear it had been contaminated with the smudgy and unwashed hands of the prior occupant. *Ew*, I could imagine Amber saying, as she handled the remote, or turned the faucet on, imagining bugs where there were only the errant stains of sporadic housekeeping. *Ew*, as she examined the wall-to-wall carpeting up close, wherein were trapped the stale scattered crumbs and souring food particles and ejaculations of a thousand prior occupants.

With Mallory dozing on and off, complaining of a migraine, I had hours to devote to my preparations. To ensure that under duress I could make the ligature knots; that I had enough Somnambulis to subdue Mallory (two purple pills, ground to a fine dust), energy drinks to maintain my vigor, and water and non-perishable snacks in the event one of my hostages became faint or dehydrated or otherwise unable to participate meaningfully in the discussion.

49

It was midsummer, the time when you and I would go on vacation. A two-week interlude in the Shawangunks, hiking the exposed rock face and helping each other through narrow crevasses. Swimming in the waters of Lake Mohonk; sitting on the porch of the mountain house after dinner, contemplating the deepening night.

I was able to make do with one valise; you with a small duffel. We slept naked in each other's arms, on an old brass bed, the crickets thrumming outside.

In the daytime we explored marked paths, routes intrepid souls had mapped (*proceed here through the glade; turn right*) so that others might enjoy the serenity of the mountains without becoming lost somewhere in the woods. Our favorite was the Labyrinth. A steep ascent, marked by faded arrows. Crevasses through which it was difficult to fit. The damp breath of the rock face. The lichens that clung, obstinately, to the undersides of things.

When we reached the summit, we called out *We are here. We are here*. Marking our presence. Claiming the ground as our own. Our voices reverberating throughout Rondout Valley. *We are here*. I, cursed with flat feet and a rear heel strike, suffered frequent blisters. You never got so much as one.

There we lingered, calling out. Neither of us in any rush to make our way back, to retrace our steps, to alight upon the path. We were at the top of the world, looking down, gazing upon the craggy faces that eons of erosion had carved from the glaciated rock of the valley.

I had found my other half, the Tristan to my Isolde. A perfect union, like Paris and Helen, or Lancelot and Guinevere. The literary and mythological antecedents too many to enumerate. I felt safe, there in your arms, as you removed my hiking boots and applied moleskin to my wounds, marveling at the tortured anatomy of my foot, fallen arches and a particularly intractable plantar wart. *What am I going to do with you?* you joked, cupping my face between your hands. The sky dissolving.

We descended in the twilight, palpating the stones, feeling our way across the rock jumble, you saving me when I lost my footing and nearly slipped into a crevasse. Were it not for your sharp reflexes, your peerless night vision, I might have dangled there uncomfortably until I could no longer hang on, surrendering to the darkness. There was a thirty-foot sheer drop, nothing to buffer a fall save for some hardy lichen. A dark end to an ignominious existence. You secured a rope around my waist and yanked me out. *Don't be scared,* you said, extending your hand, offering support, eventually carrying me on your back when my muscles gave out. We made it through the darkness, the wood, arriving finally on the shore of the gleaming lake. The moon an incandescent sliver, waning crescent.

Let's not do that again, you said. My Virgil, my guide through the underworld.

50

Amber's update indicated that you and she would be arriving at LaGuardia Airport at approximately noon the following day, assuming no unforeseen meteorological events or airline rescheduling debacles. She had posted a photo of the two of you, arms entwined, drinking from each other's hollowed-out coconuts, with the unsettling caption, *We r engaged.*

You wrote on your Facebook page that you were *falling more in love with her by the day,* that she was *the antidote to your unhappiness,* and *looked killer in a bikini. We are so in love,* you broadcast to the world, Amber lying next to you in a hammock, the sun bleeding into the water behind you. Etcetera, etcetera.

I resisted the urge to pound on the computer, to rip out the umbilicus of whatever fiber optic or cable technology was allowing me to view up-to-the-minute updates concerning your trip, inviting me into your lives, permitting me to leave inane comments, *happy for u,* my irony failing to translate in the medium.

I paced back and forth. I wandered into the bedroom, rummaged through Amber's drawers, hurling flimsy underwear and padded bras about in what might be characterized as a *frenzy.* I mangled the underwire of whatever bra lent her structured support. Ripped apart the nightgowns Amber wore to bed—filmy, transparent items that left no part of the anatomy obscured. I slashed through her size-two clothing, the items she purchased from the junior department, too small to fit into conventional sizes, even with D-cups.

I emptied jar upon jar of lotions, edible massaging creams, smearing same upon the mirror and the glass surfaces of the bathroom, the tangled scents of mint and orange blossom, the smell overpowering.

I effaced any trace of her. I turned her photos face down, so I would not have to gaze upon her countenance. Her too-white teeth, her tousled hair, the delicate mole above the upper lip. Her too-perfect nose. Her heavy-lidded eyes. *Come hither*, she beckoned the unsuspecting, the foolhardy, my husband among them.

Madge called me. "Do you want to go out tonight? There's a new band playing at Uptempo. We can catch up, and you can fill me in on your whirlwind romance with Todd!" she enthused.

If only I could, sweet Madge! If only I had heeded her pleas to *get out there*, to erase your number from the memory of my telephone, deleting the ring tone "You Are My Everything," I might not be at this critical juncture, contemplating whether the double hitch or the slipknot was more effective in subduing the average medium-weight captive. I might not be debating the morality of inducing unconsciousness in an innocent bystander.

"Ophelia, are you sure you don't want to get out? Just for a little while? It's ladies' night," Madge pleaded.

"Other plans," I replied, not wanting to get into the particulars.

"Is everything okay?" Madge asked. Evidently, she had passed by the Victorian and seen the windows boarded up, the shingles falling off, newspapers piling up on the porch.

"Haven't been home for a while," I admitted. Two weeks, to be precise, during which time I had been sleeping in your bed, retraining the patented memory foam of the mattress.

"Are you sure you're okay?" Madge inquired.

"Fine, fine," I assured her. "Seeing a lot of Todd," I said. I mentioned that he was fanatically attentive, preternaturally sensitive to my needs, possessed of superior skills in the bedroom.

"Victor was asking about you," Madge said.

"How is he?" I asked. I sensed that Madge was not entirely convinced by my tale of newfound love.

"It's a difficult transition, Ophelia," Madge said. "I just wanted to make sure you're okay."

"I'm fine. Just fine," I replied. "Going on a tour of Hudson Valley wineries this weekend," I said.

"Call if you need something, okay?"

"Will do," I assured her.

You were booked on the 8:00 a.m. flight to New York. Save for some turbulence over the Outer Banks, the flight was uneventful. Complimentary bags of cocktail peanuts all around. You touched down at LaGuardia Airport at 10:00 a.m., EST, taxiing for fifteen minutes before arriving at Gate 35.

Give or take the traffic conditions, an unforeseen accident on the Tappan Zee, a detour through Nyack, you would be arriving home around noon.

I had not yet committed any crimes. At most, I was guilty of trespass, viz., my unauthorized stay at your abode, and interference with chattel, viz., the unfortunate demise of Lulu.

There was still time to turn back. Walk out the door, *clack*, and down the garden path. I could hop in my Volvo (parked surreptitiously around the block, the license plate obscured) and make a getaway, leaving you and Amber to live out the duration of your natural lives in peace. Defriend Amber, efface any trace of myself.

T minus ninety minutes. It wasn't too late. I could still walk away with nothing more than a desk appearance ticket for trespass and aggravated harassment. So long as we keep our disturbing thoughts to ourselves; so long as we limit ourselves to writing screeds concerning our ex-husbands, we have done nothing wrong.

I went across the way to Mallory's. Told her to remain in bed, dozing, while I made breakfast. A hard-boiled egg, crisp bacon, toast, and a large glass of freshly squeezed orange juice into which I stirred the granules of Somnambulis, hoping to induce drowsiness, a pleasant state of unconsciousness (warning: the user may experience forgetfulness, loss of memory) before the subjects arrived home.

"When are Amber and Andy coming back?" she asked.

"Later today," I lied.

"I haven't tracked down the pattern yet!" she fretted.

"No need to worry," I insisted, encouraging Mallory to eat while it was warm and to drink all her orange juice, lest she succumb to vitamin deficiency. I watched nervously as she picked at the meal. Poked at the hard-boiled egg with her fork, nibbled on a strip of bacon. She took a sip of orange juice and gagged.

"Are you okay?" I asked, trying to estimate the amount she had spit out and to factor it into my calculations.

"Just went down the wrong way," she said and proceeded to empty the glass, leaving a tell-tale residue at the bottom, the faintest ring where the granules had not been thoroughly dissolved.

"Let me get you more," I insisted. Whatever qualms I had in sedating an innocent, if meddlesome bystander, I had gotten over. Whatever misgivings I had in stirring a fast-acting narcotic agent into her morning orange juice were overshadowed by the greater good. Better that she remain unconscious, unaware of what was transpiring, than to stumble into the thick of it, be drawn into our domestic turbulence, what was, after all, a matter between a man and his wife, or between a man and his wife and the mistress with whom he was now living.

Sleep well, fair Mallory, and try to avoid the disturbing dreams that are a known side effect of the prescription tranquilizer.

51

In the fall of my twenty-ninth year, I received a missive from Pensacola. The place whose coordinates I knew by heart, whose motto I could recite, whose emblem—the northern mockingbird—flitted nervously in my dreams. The place where Mother had fled, seeking a gentler clime: somewhere balmier, sunnier, better for the sinuses.

The letter was signed by someone purporting to be my sister. Mother was in the end stages of liver cancer and in great pain; none of her other daughters had proven a match for a transplant. Would I mind providing a tissue sample?

I crumpled up the letter. I declined to respond. I avoided the postman whenever he appeared at the door, attempting to obtain a signature for certified mail. I turned a deaf ear to the pleas of the transplant surgeon, a genial fellow who called to inform me that my mother would die, sooner rather than later, if a suitable match were not found. My so-called sisters were absolutely broken up. Bob beside himself.

I sat on the porch, calculating the distance between us. One thousand, one hundred ninety-four miles on Interstate 95. The vast, impregnable space. There are transgressions beyond comprehension, beyond forgiveness. The sinner who refuses to acknowledge his sins, to accept the Lord's saving graces, cannot be salvaged. He is consigned for eternity to the underworld, the place beyond hope. Virgil scolds Dante for his sympathy toward the damned, admonishing him, "Here pity, or here piety, must die."

52

August 11, 2011

A traffic snarl en route. A detour through the lovely backstreets of Valhalla. An early lunch at Milford's on the Lake, watching as the swans glided by. Two hours and one bottle of wine later, with an artful aluminum foil swan holding your leftovers (*Isn't it cute!* Amber tweeted. *A swan!*), you were on the road again.

Milford's! Where you and I had celebrated after exchanging vows before the justice of the peace. I in off-white; you in an off-the-rack suit. A handful of guests (your reluctant parents, a witness we had co-opted at city hall) joining us. We danced to a slow tempo "You Light Up My Life," gazing into one another's eyes. Your mother declared that she was happy for us. She wished us the very best as we embarked on our life together, hugging me with trepidation.

We took a walk over the footbridge and watched as the sun set over the lake. Shredded bread, throwing the cast-offs to the swans.

I love you, you said. Without caveat, without condition.

I love you too, I replied, tearing off a hunk of baguette and tossing it to the swans. Vicious sorts they, willing to poke each other's eye out for a crumb.

I heard the Fiat pull into the driveway around three o'clock. I hastened to the picture window, lifted a corner of the black-out shade, and watched. Watched as you unloaded the trunk, clutching your lower spine, moaning about having pulled something; watched as Amber lifted her halter strap, complaining about uneven tanning; watched as you tried to corral Amber's luggage on the sidewalk, the five bags she apparently thought necessary to bring for a weeklong island getaway.

I took a deep breath, summoning my strength. Hid behind the door, to capitalize on the element of surprise. One swift blow with a shovel, and I would have all the time necessary to tie you up, to ensure the fidelity of my double hitch, comparing it to the detailed illustration in *How to Make Sailors' Knots*, 5th ed.

You were the first to cross the threshold. I hesitated to bring the weapon down on your head, haunted, still, by memories of Lulu, whom I had silenced—for eternity—with more or less the same maneuver.

You had no time to react, or to register an objection. You lost consciousness and slumped to the floor.

Amber screamed, *Oh my God, don't I know you, didn't you answer the ad for the couch?*, whereupon I silenced her with a maneuver depicted in *Ninja Death Touch*, with anatomical references and warnings to apply only as much pressure as necessary to induce unconsciousness.

I knelt down beside you, ensured that you were still breathing. *I'm so sorry it had to be this way*, I apologized. It was a little late to offer *mea culpas*, but I meant it with all sincerity. I wish there had been another way. I wish you would have listened. I shook my head.

Amber was the first to awaken. Startled to find herself securely tied to a straight-backed chair, startled to see the lady she recognized as Crazyforchintz, surprise she may have had difficulty expressing due to the gag stuffed in her mouth.

She murmured something unintelligible. Something like, *What the hell is going on? What do you want from me?* Etcetera, etcetera. Twisting this way and that, thinking it possible to escape her predicament. She exhausted herself writhing and groping and grappling with the ligatures (hint: you need two hands to undo the hitch!).

"It appears it's just the two of us, dear Amber," I said. "Maybe we should get started. I don't know how much longer he'll

be out." I nodded in your direction, where you still lay unconscious, tied by a series of knots to the chair. "As you may have
guessed by now, I'm not interested in buying your chintz couch.
Do you have any idea who I am?"

She shook her head, looked around frantically.

"I'd like to remove your gag." I looked at her. "But unfortunately, I can't if you're not going to behave. Do you understand?"

Amber nodded. "Please," she whimpered. "Take whatever
you want. There's money in the bedroom, under the mattress."

"You think I want your money?" I laughed. "If all I wanted
was your money, I could have robbed you blind while you were
on your Caribbean frolic."

"What do you want then?" She was sniveling, snot streaking
down her face, mucous hanging suspensefully from one nostril.

"You're quite a mess, aren't you?" I shook my head. "And
you're getting roots," I tssked. "You're a brunette!" I exclaimed.
"You really need to cover that up."

"Please, what do you want? What have I done to you? Take
anything you want, just please untie us. We won't say anything.
Just let us go." Bargaining for time, appealing to the captor's
sympathies, assessing the feasibility of escape, should the opportunity present itself.

"What have you done? Well, now, that's an interesting question, Amber. I was going to wait for lover boy to awaken, but
maybe we should just get started. I'm sure mine is a biased
perspective," I continued. "But I think most would agree it's
bad form to steal another woman's husband, to traipse around
town holding hands while he, technically speaking, is still legally
married."

"You're—"

I allowed her tiny brain to make the intuitive leap, to arrive
at the realization that I, Crazyforchintz—the woman who had
graciously accepted one of her fliers in the parking lot outside
the mini-mart, *Lost Chihuahua, $500 reward*—was in fact your
wife, soon-to-be ex-wife.

"Yes," I confirmed. "Andy's wife, not that you cared a whit. Not that you ever stopped to consider my feelings when you were sneaking out to meet him at the Minnie Ha-Ha. Not that you ever stopped to think about me when you were prancing around in gaudy lingerie." I held up Exhibit A, the crotchless panty.

"I didn't—"

"Don't try to deny it, Amber. I followed the two of you. I saw you with my own two eyes. Checking in as Mr. and Mrs. Smith. Moaning in ecstasy. Frightening guests on family vacations. Shame on you." I paced back and forth. "And now you think you can just get engaged and everything will be fine. That you can make the past go away." I snapped my fingers in her ear. "Well, it doesn't just go away. You can't just register at Fortunoff's and think everything will be fine. You can't just walk off with my sectional furniture and think there won't be repercussions. We have to pay for our sins, Amber. Quid pro quo."

"Quid?"

"Quid pro quo. It's Latin. But I guess you never made it past ninth-grade Spanish. Not much of an intellectual, are you?" I patted her on the knee. "This for that. An equal exchange. There are many ways of restating the basic premise."

"He told me his marriage was over! That you'd drifted apart, gone your separate ways. He didn't wear a ring! He used to pick up women in the bar of the Marriott Courtyard! He flirted with the girls in the office! Why would I think he was in a committed relationship? I would never get involved with a married man! Please, please. You have to believe me."

I tried to suppress my fury. Leave it to Amber to cast doubt on your commitment! Insinuate that you were the type to troll for women at chain-hotel bars. She was trying to evade blame, deflect away from her role in the affair. "Oh, and by the way, don't think about signaling to the neighbors. They can't see you through the black-out shades. Mallory is, in any event, out of commission," I said, alluding to the drug-induced stupor the neighbor was presently sleeping off under my intermittent medical supervision.

"What have you done to her?" Amber screeched.

"You needn't concern yourself with Mallory. She'll be fine," I said. "Focus on the task at hand. Quid pro quo. Did you just think you could shack up with my husband? That there'd be no hell to pay?"

Amber remained quiet.

"There's no use denying it. There's nothing I don't know. You're sitting on my chair right now! You had your own, perfectly fine living room set, but you had to lay claim to mine. You had to take the seat out from under me, the pots from my cupboard, my espresso/cappuccino maker, the money from my pension fund…

"I hope you're proud of yourself," I spat at her, hoping to instill shame, a reflexive *hunte*, for in addition to being a despicable adultress she was greedy, always wanting more, wanting what she did not have, forcing undocumented workers to perform ingenious origami merely for the pleasure of carrying her leftovers in an aluminum foil swan, a swan she would casually tear open and roll into a ball, without a care for their labors, the fifty steps necessary merely to make a convincing-looking wing-fold.

"Cat got your tongue?" I elbowed her. "You're usually so chatty. Usually so eager to share every detail. Especially on Facebook. Oh, I truly enjoy your postings. Every aspect of your romantic idyll. Hang-gliding, parasailing, an over-the-water bungalow, spare no expense on my account. Aren't the dolphins cute? Tell me, did they evacuate Flipper to the indoor enclosure before the hurricane made landfall?"

"Can I have some water?" Amber pleaded.

"Oh, did you not eat enough at Milford's on the Lake? I thought their portions were quite generous."

"How do you know—"

"Really, Amber? You have 5,000 friends. You broadcast every moment of your life. You're suffering from overexposure.

Shall we examine your feed now? Oh, you've been uncharacteristically silent for more than an hour… Should we post something? Just arrived home and looking forward to a quiet night
at home!"

Amber shook her head. "What do you want?" she sniffled.

"Now you're suddenly concerned with what I want?" I re-
joined. "You didn't seem at all concerned when you were seducing my husband, buying him drinks at the Hula Bar at the
Holiday Inn, proposing that you have a 'good time, no strings
attached.'

"Yes, dear Amber, I am privy to your electronic communications. Damning evidence, it is." I reviewed a few excerpts:

Meet me at Mini Ha-Ha [*sic*] *in one hour.*

Are my breasts too big for you [really, Amber?] *Maybe I should get
a reduction. They kinda hurt my back.*

Let's go skinny dipping in the pool after midnight!

I left you a present [i.e., aromatic crotchless panties] *in the glove
compartment!*

"He was admittedly quite taken with you. Impressed with
your sexual verve. Though he did mention some stretch marks
on your thighs. Did you used to be fat, dear Amber? Shunned
as a teenager? Too much of you to love? Do you have a terrible
need to overcompensate? To take iPhone pictures in skimpy
underwear? Proving to yourself once and for all that you are a
desirable woman?

"Nothing to say? How uncharacteristic." I allowed Amber
a few sips from a water bottle. Turned on the air conditioner
so as to alleviate the sweating and itching occasioned by her
bindings. Alternated *gag in, gag out*, so that her mouth did not
dry out. I showed her mercy, though she had displayed none
for me, seducing my husband, wooing him with her Frederick's of Hollywood charms, leading him down the path to Hell,
where Charon, the ferryman, awaits (scholars have long noted
the overlay of Greek mythological figures in what is otherwise
the *echt* Judeo-Christian depiction of Hell, the place where sin-

ners are systemically punished according to the severity of their offenses).

"What do you have to say for yourself? Any reflections?" I prodded. "Very well. I have to say, I'm disappointed. I'd thought we could have a more productive dialogue. It's not going to be very fun if all you do is sit there, hanging your head. Are you even sorry? Sorry in the least for stealing my husband?"

"I didn't mean to hurt you. You have to believe me," she whimpered. "I didn't plan on getting involved with him. I wasn't even attracted to him at first. It just happened. One thing led to another. He made me laugh." (What she left unsaid: they fornicated in a seedy motor court off Route 1 with thin walls and a tacky steamboat motif, passing themselves off as Mr. and Mrs. Smith.)

"Enough!" I screamed, my voice hoarse from the exchange. "Do you think that absolves you? That you're blameless?"

"I'm sorry. I'm really sorry we hurt you," she sobbed.

She claimed to have had a drink with you, quite innocently, one night after work. According to her, you were instantly smitten. You actively pursued her. You asserted that you had never met a woman like her. Life until that point had been nothing more than a series of boring cadaver demonstrations and unfulfilling relationships. Albeit technically married, you assured her that the wife (i e , me) would pose no impediment to your relationship. *Men just like me.* Amber shrugged, a convenient excuse for adulterous activities in family friendly establishments like the Minnie Ha-Ha.

"We can't willfully ignore things, and then profess our innocence." Hell is filled with virtuous pagans, disbelievers, even unbaptized babies. "Look at me," I directed. "Do you think it's easy to start over at the age of forty? To meet people on Our Time? Geriatric widowers, fifty-year-olds who've never been married and still live with their mothers?" I asked, recalling the latest inquiries I'd received in response to my online dating profile. "Do you think you can run off with my husband, play with dolphins, prance around in gaudy underwear, no thought whatsoever to my well-being? To the havoc you've created?"

Amber sniffled. "I'm sorry. Please, please, just let me go. I'm really uncomfortable. I need to go to the bathroom," she said. "Please, can you just untie me for a minute? I don't want to pee in my pants."

"I have little sympathy," I said. While she was sleeping on memory foam, I was curled in a ball in the basement. While she was using a flush toilet, I was voiding in buckets. While she was nestling in the crook of your arm, I was sleeping in the pitch dark on a hard and cold floor, feeling cockroaches on the surface of my skin.

While she was posting on Facebook, rhapsodizing about her newfound love, I was moldering inside an old Victorian, watching *Snapped* and *Hoarders*, gorging on Chunky Monkey, caring not a whit about my appearance or my life. If you were gone, nothing was left for me. Nothing but hollowed-out memories, unsightly scars, tissue formations that would never heal.

"Did he give you this?" I removed the engagement ring from her finger. "Let me guess, two carats? We'd find a lot of flaws if we held it under the light, I'm sure." I hurtled it against the kitchen cabinet, where it scored the wood veneer. "Oops, sorry.

"Don't cry, Amber. It's just a thing. A symbol. Oh, look now, your makeup is running. You've got raccoon eyes," I tssked. "Oh yes, where were we?" I resumed. "We were just discussing regrets. Whether you're sorry, truly sorry, for having hurt me. For stealing my husband. For emptying my house and its contents."

"What do you want me to say?" she heaved. "Sorry, sorry, sorry. I shouldn't have had a drink with him. I shouldn't have fallen for him. I shouldn't have let him move in. I shouldn't have taken your couch or your juicer or your cappuccino maker. Now, please, let me go!"

"Forgive me, but I'm not quite convinced of the sincerity of your apology." She who had fornicated with my husband at the Minnie Ha-Ha, not even bothering to close the musty blinds.

She who pranced around in neon green thong, jiggling for all the world to see. She who blithely suggested, *Why don't you move in, we're always together anyway?*, unconcerned about the wife he was leaving behind, alone to brood in the house, watching *Hoarders*. She who had forced the wife to resort to the taking of captives and the drugging of intermeddling neighbors merely so she could make her points.

"God, he said you were crazy and he wasn't kidding!" she screamed.

"I'm afraid we're going in circles now, not getting anywhere. I've given you every chance to make a sincere apology, but you evidently think you have nothing to apologize for. You might want to rethink your perspective," I counseled her.

I paused. I took a moment to slake my thirst and to work out the cramps in my fingers, gnarled from having to make so many knots. She had hurt me; I would hurt her in turn, quid pro quo. "By the way, now that we're having this heart-to-heart, there's something I ought to tell you." I hesitated. "Lulu's not coming back. She's never coming back."

Amber's eyes widened.

"It really couldn't be helped. She wouldn't stop barking. I'd only meant to silence her, but unfortunately it appears I inflicted a fatal head injury."

I regretted mentioning the subject. Whatever her finicky quirks, however godawful her yapping, Lulu did not deserve to die. She did not deserve to be *thwacked* over the head and buried in shallow fill. She was an innocent. A fluffy toy breed. A creature who deserved more than an undignified and hasty burial.

"You're a monster!" Amber screamed. "A monster," she managed, before I was obliged to silence her, shoving the gag in her mouth.

I took a moment to check on Mallory. I failed to look in both directions as I crossed the street and was nearly sideswiped by a passing vehicle. "Look where you're going!" The driver shook his hand at me, failing to appreciate the mental duress under which I was operating, the state of deep concentration required lest I slip up, fail to secure a knot, or miscalculate the dosage of Somnambulis necessary to subdue a slightly overweight woman of average height.

"Watch where you're going!" I shouted, but he was already outside of earshot.

Peering in the bedroom, I ascertained that Mallory was, in fact, sleeping comfortably, respiring regularly. I disconnected the ringer on her telephone so that she did not awaken from sleep with a start; I turned off the television so as to avoid her startling to the familiar theme music to *Hoarders*, to awaken in time for the season four marathon. *Sleep well, fair Mallory, and come the morn, I shall be gone.* I blotted the cheek where her saliva had pooled, propping her on her side so as to facilitate sinus drainage. *Sorry to have involved you, to have sent you on wild goose chases around the tri-state area in search of discontinued china patterns. By the way, my name is Ophelia, not Patty, as I might have led you to believe. Amber and I are not "like sisters," as I may have represented, but more like mortal enemies, engaged in a struggle to the death for limited resources.*

I left and went back across the street. "I'm home," I announced.

Amber had somehow managed, despite alleged cramping occasioned by being in a stress position for hours, to hop across the room and nearly make it to the landline. She had evidently not puzzled through how, after thumping across the floor, she would dial the telephone (given that her hands were bound) or shout into the receiver (given the gag in her mouth, impeding her ability to speak).

"Amber, Amber," I tssked. "How do you expect me to trust you? Five minutes and you can't keep still?" I disconnected the telephone and threw it down the stairs, where it landed with a *thud.*

You awoke with a start.

"Oh, nice of you to join the land of the living, Andy. We've been waiting forever," I said, removing the duct tape from your mouth, giving you a chance to express your thoughts.

"What the hell is going on?" you asked, looking around. "What are you doing here?"

"I am still, technically, your wife. At least for the next week or so, until, by operation of law, our marriage is dissolved as per Section 10 of the Domestic Relations Law. You're not looking well," I said. "I thought you were on a beach holiday. Why do you look so poorly rested? I thought swimming with dolphins helped to restore the 'vital energies' depleted by modern life?"

Amber shook her head.

"Sorry to burst in on you like this but I'm afraid we have some unfinished business. Things that need sorting out. It's difficult to know where to begin. I've been getting to know your girlfriend," I said, pointing to where Amber sat bound, drooling, the gag stuffed in her mouth.

"You're fucking crazy!" you snarled at me.

"Is it crazy to defend what's mine? To expect you to act with a modicum of decency? To presume, upon exchanging vows, that you would stand by me, and not run off with, with…" I pointed to Amber. Identifying, by my gesture, the agent of sin. The provider of illicit pleasures in by-the-hour motels.

"You're not going to get away with this."

"With what? I'm just trying to have a conversation. A dialogue. A productive exchange. Something I've been precluded from doing by virtue of the restraining order." I may have tied and bound you and your paramour, but you had effectively silenced me via entry of a so-called stay away order of protection.

"What are you trying to accomplish?" You shook your head. You insinuated that I was unable to accept reality. You asserted that I was living in my own fantasy world, unable to register the fact that we were no longer together. *The marriage shall be dissolved, nunc pro tunc, as if it never existed.* You said there was no point in talking, since you had long ago arrived at the conclusion that I was deficient in some essential way that precluded meaningful lifelong commitment. You maintained that Amber filled a void, *a void* as you called it; I, whether due to past traumas or other intractable flaws (a perpetually gloomy disposition, a sour view of human nature), was incapable of being the upbeat and perennially optimistic spouse you deserved. I was precluded from approaching within one hundred feet of you, or communicating with you save through the intermediary of our respective counselors-at-law; I had, therefore, committed some gross violation by tying you and Amber up, impeding your physical movement, actions that might be construed as kidnapping or false imprisonment under the relevant statutes.

"You've been under her spell." I nodded in Amber's direction. You were unable to see the light, operating under the belief, mistaken, that you were in love, when in fact you were merely infatuated, temporarily diverted, blinded by her charms.

"Do you disagree?" I asked Amber. She shook her head.

"I knew you were up to something," you asserted. "You've been following me, haven't you? I knew I spotted you. You're not getting away with this."

"Who's being paranoid now?" I shot back. I may have, on one or two occasions, followed you to the juncture of Routes 1 and 2, watched as you arrived at the offices of Halford Medical Supply, lugging your suitcase of supplies and your simulation cadaver. I may have followed you on certain sales calls, watching with interest as you demonstrated the Penetrate-R laparoscope, useful for boring through the skin of even the most overweight patients. I may have watched you hurriedly stuff a burger deluxe with onion rings into your mouth at the diner off the highway, rushing to the next call, but I most certainly had *not* been following you in the manner suggested. Not in any kind of way that would imply regular and/or systematic tracking of your movements.

"Why can't you just leave us alone? Get on with your life, Ophelia," you sighed, apparently not appreciating the untenable position in which you had placed me, your wife, by consorting with and ultimately leaving me for the vixen Amber Halloway.

"I'm not the one who broke my marriage vows. I'm not the one who invented out-of-town trips and doctored expense reports. I'm not the one who proposed to someone else before

the ink was even dry on the divorce papers." For you had reneged on our pact. Left me alone in a drafty house with memories I'd spent the better part of decades trying to repress. Awake
at night, dissecting explanations, wondering whether you were
truly in Cincinnati at the Midwest medical supply convention,
as represented, or whether you were shacked up with Amber
in the motor court. Biding my time, gorging on Ben & Jerry's,
wondering when, or if, you might return. Wondering what I had
done to alienate your affections; why you spent an inordinate
amount of time on the road, driving from convention to convention, a gallon of embalming fluid and a simulation cadaver
in the trunk of your rental car.

"Well, I'm not the one skulking around town in a beat-up
Volvo, pretending not to be following people. I'm not the one
hacking into accounts and intercepting electronic communica
tions. I'm not the one committing identity theft," you coun
tered. "I'm not making sick photoshopped collages of Amber's
body parts—" You winced, recalling an admittedly tasteless
gesture when first I'd found out that you were cheating on me.

"I am *not* skulking around town. I have kept very much to
myself, hardly venturing outside." I omitted to mention that I
had, in fact, been camped out in the abandoned and soon-to-
be foreclosed-upon Lark property for the last three months.
Sleeping in a basement, watching you through a viewfinder, as
if in the crosshairs I might finally ascertain *why* you had left, the
illuming moment when everything would make sense.

"And what are you doing now? Taking hostages? Impris-
oning us?" You were sweating profusely despite the air condi-
tioning, your face unduly red. A deep line between your brows,
a signifier of worry and vexation. You'd often counseled me
against brooding, warning that it was bad for the physiognomy,
leading to brow creases and crow's feet, the breakdown of the
collagen substrate.

"I'm just trying to have a conversation," I huffed. If only you
would stop insisting that you had seen me at the intersection of
Oak and Willow Streets, in dark glasses and wig, and grant me a

minute. If only you would stop hurling hurtful terms like *stalker* and *borderline personality disorder* around—watching marathons of *Snapped* had apparently rendered you an expert in psychiatric disorders—we might get somewhere.

You might see, perhaps, that we were destined to be together. Amber a diversion; you and I the real thing. I Guinevere; you Lancelot. Your scars healed; mine thick keloids. Our words reverberating off the rock face, *I love you, I love you.* I would forever serve gladly as your surgical dummy.

"You're going to do time for this," you huffed.

"And what about you? How will you pay for what you've done?"

"What *I've* done? What have I done? I don't want to be with you anymore. I filed for divorce. It's not a crime. Do you think obsessively following me and reading my private emails makes me want to be with you?"

"I did not set out to read your email," I harrumphed. Leaving your computer untended might be construed by some as an invitation to rummage through electronic files. Or at least not a disincentive. It's only because I stumbled on correspondence referring to rendezvous at the Minnie Ha-Ha that you were so indignant. I still remember the subject line: *It's so warm inside of you.*

"And you." I pointed at Amber. "How can you proclaim to be innocent? You were meeting him at the Minnie Ha-Ha. Registered under assumed names." She had aided and abetted his marital transgressions. She had given him salacious encouragement, hastening the dissolution of the marriage and the mental decline, if not certifiable breakdown, of one of its participants. She could not profess to be innocent.

"Don't blame her, Ophelia," you retorted, ever so chivalrously. You shouldered the entirety of the blame, berating yourself for letting matters *get out of hand*, for failing to be honest with me about your feelings for Amber and your desire to extricate yourself from what you termed a *lackluster marriage.* You hadn't meant to stray, but you were bored, feeling too keenly the onus of *forever*. You'd once been vibrant, and now you were sitting on a couch, watching reruns of *Hoarders*, familiar with every variety of collector obsession (Tupperware, Santas, garden gnomes, Madame Alexander dolls). You longed to feel *alive*. You longed to be *free*. You wanted to make love in broad daylight with someone who wasn't self-conscious about her *body flaws*. It was you who had seduced Amber during the Midwest medical supply convention. You who proposed returning to room 542 to have some fun. You who ravished her on the plaid bedspread, casting her panties aside, finding yourself *unbelievably aroused*, silencing your phone for the duration, ignoring the wife's plaintive calls, oblivious to her pain, her need to know where you were at all times lest she unnecessarily obsess over the prospect of you leaving. "It was my fault." You hung your head. "Blame me."

"Please," Amber mumbled. Her gag was slipping. "Just let us go." She had mascara smudges under her eyes. Eyes crackling with red filaments.

"My family said you were crazy. They said not to marry you. She's too damaged, they said. But, no, I wouldn't listen."

She's too damaged, presumably a reference to my inauspicious circumstances: to my brooding father, dead by self-administered shotgun wound; to the mother who abandoned me one day without explanation, never looking back, at least not until diagnosed with terminal cancer and left to wonder about how she had conducted her life, whether she had any regrets, regrets like leaving behind an impressionable eight-year-old for whom she was the entire world, *clack*, steps in the gravel rut.

She's too damaged. An acknowledgment that certain events having transpired, the human being is scarred in irremediable ways, beyond rehabilitation, beyond the therapeutic acumen of most mental health professionals, beyond the help of commercially available anti-anxiety medications, *Why did you leave me? I hate you*, blows absorbed by cushioning foam pillows, stand-ins for those who have done us harm.

"What do they know about me?" I screamed. "They didn't even stay for the reception. They gave us a punch bowl."

"They knew our marriage was doomed. I was just too bull-headed to be talked out of it."

I kicked you in the shin. "I'm not in the mood to listen to your diatribes," I sighed. "You've been calling the shots for too long. Doing as you please, fornicating at the Minnie Ha-Ha—the Minnie Ha-Ha for God's sake!"—while I fretted, home alone, thinking you had been run off the highway. Thinking I'd get a call that you'd been in an accident. That you'd run into a tree on the bend. That you'd had a few too many and gone the wrong way down the road. That you'd failed to anticipate a curve and catapulted over the guardrail, rolled down the hill, and became trapped inside a flaming vehicle, unable to extricate yourself from imminent disaster.

Having a mother who took off one day, without a note or an explanation, I was understandably apprehensive every time a loved one left, purporting to go on an errand or to fill up the gas tank. Trying to discern, in the words, *I'll just be gone a minute, see you soon,* an unmistakable clue, a quaver in the voice, a tremolo that would give them away. For the human heart must somehow betray itself, reveal its intentions.

"How could you, Andy? How could you betray me? Leave me without warning?" I had fortified myself for the encounter with a glass of whiskey and a liberal dose of anti-anxiety medication, not wanting to appear nervous or to let emotions get the better of me. Emotions I thought I had wrangled into submission, or at least sufficiently compartmentalized.

I foundered. Broke down, sobbing. Tears streaked down my face. I tried to wipe them with the sleeve of my frayed and threadbare tracksuit. They dripped, *plop-plop, splat,* onto the floor. I had difficulty catching my breath.

"Look." You softened. "I know I haven't done right by you. I shouldn't have been sneaking around. I should have been honest with you. I just thought you couldn't handle it. I wanted to spare you. You were always good to me. Always a very loving wife. You kept me afloat during sales lulls. You understood what it took to get ahead in the competitive northeastern market. You remembered to keep the pantry stocked with cocoa puffs." You went on, enumerating the ways in which I had been a loving and devoted spouse. "You didn't deserve to be treated that way."

I regarded you with a dubious eye.

"I did love you, Ophelia. I really did. Just maybe not the way you loved me. Just maybe not the way you needed. I wish I would have done things differently. I wish I hadn't been so selfish, so insensitive to your feelings. You didn't deserve to be treated that way. I should have been honest. I shouldn't have misled you about what was going on. I wish I could take it back. It's my fault, really."

"He's telling the truth! He never wanted to hurt you," Amber interjected, mascara dripping down her cheeks.

I wanted to believe you. I wanted to believe that you were sorry, *truly sorry*, for running off with the vixen Amber Halloway, for leaving me alone, nothing to remember you by save an obsolete surgical robot and a few straggling items in the closet. For making off with the espresso/cappuccino maker, leaving me with a crock pot and a jar of Sanka. For claiming entitlement to half my retirement benefits, while disavowing altogether any association with me. For erasing me from your life.

"Yes, yes. I was selfish. Thinking only of myself. Taking the easy way out. Can you forgive me?"

Your speech was touching. Seemingly heart-felt. Still, I could not help feeling that you were not being entirely honest, that your "apology" was nothing more than a cynical ploy to gain your freedom. You were, after all, a salesman par excellence, with no compunction about pawning off last year's model upon unsuspecting hospital buyers, none about selling *samples, not for resale*, to doctors you encountered on the road. You were simply stalling, buying time, increasing the chances that a neighbor or friend might stumble upon us, draw the obvious conclusions, and alert the authorities.

"Stop talking." I paced back and forth, working off nervous energy. I peered outside, ensuring that there was no police activity afoot. The bank inspectors had boarded up the Lark property, interring within the telescope and the last of my provisions.

There was no going back. No curling myself in a ball and falling asleep on a cement floor. No eking out water from an erratic faucet. No peeing into gallon-size containers I'd later dump in the yard.

I'd revealed myself. Shown myself to be hurt, to be damaged, to be harboring negative and even explosive emotions. We would not be returning to Lake Mohonk; we would never be returning. Our words echoing off the rock face.

"You're not thinking straight. I know you're angry, you have every right to be," you conceded. "But there are better ways to work through our problems, aren't there?" Ways, presumably, that did not involve restraining mistresses and drugging neighbors and recording lengthy observations, in cramped penmanship, of life observed through a telescope.

"If you think on it, you'll realize I'm right. Look, just untie us and we can forget all about it." You rubbed the side of your head, the place where I had thwacked you with a shovel. "I won't tell anyone if you won't." You smiled, the same way you smiled at doctors to whom you were demonstrating the agility of the Penetrate-R laparoscope, *enables you to get right in there, less surgical trauma*, the same way you had smiled at me, brushed a hair from my face and assured me that you were not having an affair with Miss Amber Halloway, I was crazy for thinking otherwise.

"Forgive me if I'm disbelieving," I said, pacing back and forth, wearing a tread in the pile carpeting.

"Ophelia, you know I'm right. I'm just trying to help out here."

"Don't patronize me!" I snapped. I ripped open the foil swan and gnawed on the overcooked beef *bourguignon*. "Sorry to eat your leftovers, Amber. But I need my energy," I explained, as if I needed to explain anything to her, she who had no compunction whatsoever about stealing my husband.

"Look, we can stay and talk for hours. Just let Amber go,"
you pleaded. "She has nothing to do with it."

"Please," I scoffed. "You think I don't see what you're trying
to do? You think I'm that stupid?" The beef, in red wine reduction, was not half-bad.

"Of course not. It's just—"

"Just what?" I shook my head. "You brought her to Milford's, Andy! Is nothing sacred?" We danced to "You Light Up
My Life." We fed each other a slice of wedding cake; we promised it would be forever.

After your parents made their exit (they needed to be back
in Hastings-on-the-Hudson by sundown; your father's field of
vision was narrowing and soon would be gone), we wandered
onto the footbridge. We gazed upon the swans gliding by. We
threw them crumbs from our wedding cake. Golden sponge
and buttercream icing.

They circled back for more. Looked at us, clucking, as if to
say, *toss me another crumb*. Waded on shore and approached us.
Their black mouths devouring. Their honk nasal and not in the
least mellifluous.

"I shouldn't have brought her there," you conceded. "Now
can you let us go?" you snapped, trying to cut off any productive dialogue. "I love her, Ophelia. I know you don't want to
hear it, but I do. I love her, and I'm going to marry her [Amber
shaking her head, clattering the chair]. She's the best thing that
ever happened to me, and we're going to be together [Amber's
eyes opening wide], no matter how many knots you tie me up in
or how many times you try to convince me I made a mistake by
leaving you. It was not a mistake," you declaimed, displaying no
contrition, no *honte*, but a monstrous self-regard and a bedevil-
ing indifference to the sufferings of others.

It was hopeless. I could see that now. There was no turning
back. No prospect of a tearful reconciliation. None of renewing our vows; of sitting on the porch swing, hand in hand, listening to the cicadas. None of sleeping, nestled in one another,
shielded from the world and its caprices. None of awakening in

each other's arms, opening the blinds, and gazing upon the day. The cupolas were flaking; the floorboards creaking; pigeons had taken up residence in the attic and refused to be evicted.

We would not be returning to the mountain house. We would not be scrambling up the Labyrinth, helping each other through the narrow crevasses. We would not, upon reaching the summit, be sharing the lunch that congenial folk from the hotel kitchen had packed for us. Toast with crunchy peanut butter; a half carafe of wine we'd uncork with a Swiss Army knife. We would not be enjoying our repast from our perch overlooking Roundout Valley and the glacial lake below. *We are here.*

We would not be renewing our vows, consecrating ourselves to one another for eternity. We would not be resuming marital affections, even after the order of protection had expired. For you were in love with Amber.

Abandon all hope, ye who enter here.

I may have upset the vase on the coffee table. I may have flung a plate, or two, or three, from the cupboards, leaving shards on the floor. I may have shouted an expletive or two, letting it be known that you were going to Hell, if only the second circle, for sins of carnal lust.

You had wounded me; I would wound you in return. You had driven a stake into my heart (figuratively); I would inflict pain (literally). My own form of retributive justice.

As they torment in life, they will be so tormented in death. The lovers who scoff at conventions and defy all social mores, will in Hell be denied fulfillment. Forever to gaze upon, but never to possess one another.

Quid pro quo. I had tried to explain it to Amber. If the law no longer saw fit to criminalize adultery, adopting expansive notions of "no fault" divorce, I would act as the agent of justice, exacting punishment.

"Wait a minute," you panicked. "You're not going to hurt us. I know you won't hurt us, please don't do anything, Ophelia, please, I'm begging you," you said, abandoning the veneer of the skilled negotiator, of the cloying salesperson looking to close a deal, showing yourself to be nothing more than a blubbering coward, a spineless charlatan, a man of no substance whatsoever. "She has a heart condition!" you screeched.

"Please, Andy. You're just embarrassing yourself now." I chewed off the last scrap of beef, twirling the swan's foil neck in my hand, the many silver leaves that had been carefully woven to replicate the arched neck.

"I'm not kidding! It's somewhere in the luggage. In a carry-on bag. I'm telling you. She takes digitalis."

Amber whimpered.

"You expect me to rifle through five bags of luggage?" I asked, incredulous. "In the time it would take me to do that, you'd be halfway to Mexico. Ever think of packing more lightly?" I nudged Amber.

"Please, just let her go. She can't handle too much stress."

"Your concern is touching," I said. Eminently fearful of inducing an erratic heartbeat in Miss Amber Halloway, yet caring not a whit about causing me pain, instigating mental instability, reawakening traumas, recalling for me the unfortunate circumstances of my mother's leave-taking. My well-being, my day-to-day functioning, my mental health, meaningless. My ability to go on, to assimilate the fact that you had cheated on me, not once or twice, but repeatedly, openly, and notoriously, in a motor court just off the throughway with the derisive name *Minnie Ha-Ha*.

"You have me. Isn't that what you wanted? We're here together. We're talking things through. Getting to see one another's perspective. Come on, Ophelia," you pleaded, a desperate quaver in your voice. "She doesn't need to be here. Please, Ophelia. Think of all the good times we had. I want to cherish all those memories. Here." You put a hand over your heart.

Appealing to the times we shared, just the two of us, hiking up the mountain face, watching the last light of day disintegrate, fall apart. Walking through the forest, twigs snapping underfoot, the loon calling out, your hand gripping mine, telling me, *It will be all right. I'm here now. I'm not going anywhere. I'm not going anywhere.*

Time is not linear, but a tripwire, events we keep stumbling over, again and again, nettles in the brain, thorns in the heart.

"Don't you dare. Don't you DARE," I shouted. "Don't you DARE bring up the past."

"She's OUT!" you screamed, purporting to be horrified, hopping over for a closer look.

"She's fine," I assured you.

"We need to call an ambulance," you insisted. "Please."

"She's perfectly fine," I asserted. Her pulse strong, her color vibrant, her breaths shallow, but nothing alarming.

"She's fading. Please. Can you at least get her medication?"

"You expect me to rummage through five suitcases?" I sighed, exasperated at the lengths you expected me to go through in furtherance of the charade. "Fine." I humored you. The first case was filled entirely with skin and hair products. "She's high maintenance, isn't she?" I tssked.

"Untie me," you begged. "I can help."

"You're not going anywhere," I said. The second and third bags contained swimsuits and lingerie in every conceivable color and tawdry style, sheer blouses, wispy cover-ups, enough to fill the Frederick's of Hollywood catalog. "You must have paid through the nose in luggage fees."

"We don't have time for this!" you insisted.

"I'm sorry. But I'm the one calling the shots here. I've been kind enough to indulge you, to give you the benefit of the doubt. What kind of heart condition can she have, for God's sake? She works out on a trampoline. She kickboxes on Tuesdays and Fridays. Not to mention your vigorous sex life." I shook my head, disgusted. The indignity of having to rummage through Amber's luggage, to discover, amid the silk underthings and the sordid panties and the cheetah teddy, underneath *Tantric Sex, One Thousand Positions to Ecstasy* (illustrated), and the

glow-in-the-dark condoms (x-tra, x-tra large), a letter, on hotel
stationery, in which you professed the following:

*Amber, will you marry me? I will make you happy forever. Please say
yes, and I will be the happiest man on the planet!*

I stuffed the note in the garbage disposal (ignoring your
plaintive protests, *there's no time!*), made myself a gin and tonic,
and sat down, hoping to catch my breath.

"We have to DO SOMETHING," you screamed.

"Let's hold on a minute." I put my feet up on the table. "I've
indulged you. I've looked through the luggage in search of the
elusive 'heart medication,' to no avail. I think I'm entitled to a
drink or two. It's been an exhausting day. Are you sure you don't
want a drink?"

"I'm SURE," you shouted.

"I'm sorry, but you're giving me a headache." I tore off a
piece of duct tape and secured it over your mouth.

I might (as the prosecutor underscored in summation) have
made a more thorough search of Amber's luggage. Instead of
confining myself to the main compartments, which contained a
bounty of colorful lingerie and shape-affirming undergarments,
I might have taken a moment to explore the side pockets. Instead of declaring the search *over* after traipsing through the
lurid teddies and boned corsets, after running across the Tantric
sex manuals and the disturbing personal massaging device, I
might have dug deeper into the corners. Therein I might have
found, if I had been so inclined, an amber bottle of twenty
pills, to be taken at regular intervals, preferably on a full stomach with a glass of water.

Would have, should have, could have. The refractive possibilities.
The paths down which we might have otherwise been deflected.

53

Long before I had anticipated, Mallory appeared on the doorstep with a supersize bag of ridged chips and sour cream dip. She informed me that the *Hoarders* marathon—all fifteen episodes, back-to-back, with limited commercial interruption—was about to start.

I warned her that the place was in disarray; that I had been stricken with food poisoning after chancing to eat at the Jack-in-the-Box; that, unable to make it to the bathroom in time, I had regurgitated on the carpet.

"You don't feel well, hon?" She put a hand to my forehead. "You are feeling clammy. And you're kind of pale."

"After throwing up, I feel so depleted. I ought to just get to bed."

"I can help you. If you're feeling too weak. It's the least I can do."

"I truly appreciate your concern, but I can manage. It's still messy back there, I haven't had a chance to clean it up. I'd be awfully embarrassed if you stumbled upon—"

"No need to be embarrassed!" she exclaimed. She insisted on reciprocating my acts of neighborly hospitality, on tending to me in my besmirched state—a kindness, under any other circumstances, that I would have appreciated.

"Just trying to gather my strength before the lucky couple returns. Leave the place as I found it, clean the mess off the bathroom floor—" I was babbling, admittedly, and desperate to be rid of Mallory, for her to turn back, to cross the street, to distance herself from me, association with whom could lead to no good end.

"Why are you so eager to get rid of me?" she asked. "It's not like you." She pushed against the door. Not hard, but enough, apparently, to catch a glimpse of you in the background. Hopping across the floor, banging against the cabinetry, trying to attract attention. "Andy? Is that you?"

If only I had resisted her more forcefully. Yawned and told her that I was in no condition for visitors, doubled over from stomach cramps, and slammed the door in her face.

She burst in. Took in the scene, viz., Amber tied to the chair, a gag stuffed in her mouth. The five ransacked suitcases of luggage on the living room floor (I told her I needed to tidy up!). "You need to go," I said, thinking, somehow, that I could still persuade her to be gone, to distance herself from the domestic melodrama transpiring.

"What's going on? What's going on? Quick, we need to call 911!"

The landline was unfortunately out-of-service, its internal mechanisms hopelessly smashed.

"Give me your cell phone!" Mallory screamed, referring to me still as *Patty*, still under the apprehension, apparently, that I was nothing more than an innocent house sitter. It had not yet dawned on her that *I* was the one who had stunned them using a shovel, *I* who had tied the knots and secured the restraints, the double hitch effectively impossible to undo.

"She's barely breathing," Mallory screamed, crouched by Amber, pressing her ear to her chest.

"911. What is your emergency?"

"My neighbor is unconscious!" Mallory screeched. "I can't find her pulse." She began chest compressions. *One-two-three-four-five*, beseeching Amber's heart to respond. *One-two-three-four-five*. I watched from a distance, floating outside myself. The same way my soul would wander, when, as a little girl, I had cried past the point of feeling, no longer able to sense myself or my body. *One-two-three-four-five*. No longer hampered by the physical, the wretched pain of the human condition.

"Hold tight, ma'am, emergency medical services is en route."

One-two-three-four-five. Sweat poured down Mallory's brow. "Don't just stand there," she screeched at me where I stood frozen. "Untie Andy, for God's sake." She continued pressing down on Amber's chest, pausing now and again to listen for a breath, an inspiration, a weak gag that would at least be indicative of basic brain stem reflexes, but Amber was unresponsive.

"She's not responding!" Mallory screamed.

"Calm down, ma'am. Help is on the way."

"Untie him, for God's sake! Snap out of it!" she screamed.

Click. Steps down a gravel path. And nothing is ever the same again. The timbre of the wind, the smell of wet earth, the warm space in my mother's neck, everything I had ever known.

"What's wrong with you?" *One-two-three-four-five*. Mallory had watched enough medical reenactment shows to know when life-saving procedures were futile. "Wake up!" she nonetheless screeched at Amber. "Wake up!"

Mallory collapsed sobbing. If I had any sense, if I were thinking clearly, I would have slipped out the door, never looking back. I would have taken advantage of the confusion—*check her pulse!*—to slip out undetected, to get in the car and drive somewhere far, far away, somewhere I could subsist off the land, live under a false name, evade the interstate warrant they would be sure to issue for my arrest once my role in the kidnapping had been made clear.

Standing there, I threw up. Chunks of beef *bourguignon* in a red wine reduction.

"Did *you* do this? Did you?" Mallory pointed a finger at me. Watching true crime stories and homicide reenactments had alerted her to the darkness lurking within the human heart.

I said nothing.

"Of course! It was you!" she exclaimed, the viewfinder coming into focus. The sudden appearance of the houseguest, one day, without forewarning or explanation. The unexplained blackouts, the sense of time unaccounted for, the strange aftertaste of bitters. Waking up in her bed the morning after with dry mouth, a nagging headache, and the sense that something was amiss, something she could not pinpoint.

"Why?" she asked, uncomprehending. "Why?"

The approach of sirens. Ten minutes, not a bad response

time for Saratoga County. The rush of footsteps. Directives to
get down on the ground, not to move. The feel of metal on my
wrists, *click*, the circle closing.

*It's my ex wife. She did it! She killed her. She killed her. Took us
hostage. Refused to let us go. I told her my fiancée suffered from a heart
condition! I told her! She knew. There's digitalis in the suitcase, in the side
compartment.* You retrieved the bottle, the capsules that might
have saved her—had I, in traipsing through the luggage, not
become unduly distracted by the underwear and the sex toys
and the degrading evidence of your infidelities.

See? It was there the whole time. She let her die! you screamed,
pointing the finger at me, sprawled face down on the floor,
hands behind my back, my view obstructed. *She refused to untie
her. I was begging her!* You sobbed, hovering over Amber's body,
stroking her hair, intoning her name, summoning every tender-
ness. Howling as the coroner took her away on his collapsible
gurney.

You may want to look away, the coroner said, as he zipped up
the black bag and wheeled Amber into the night.

They ushered me into the back seat of a police vehicle. Informed me that I was being taken into custody on charges of
felony murder and kidnapping, the words like stones skipping
across the water. I sat in the vehicle, gazing out the window. The
glass smudged, distorted. Taking in the scene. *She killed her!* you
mouthed, pointing the finger at me. *It was her!* you screamed,
ensuring that the identity of the culprit was known. Your pain
audible through double-glazed windows, through sound-proof
glass.

"I'm sorry," I murmured.

I might (as the prosecutor underscored in summation) have
found more constructive outlets for my pain. Joined a reading
group, taken up knitting, done a better job of persuading pro
spective dates that I was a sane, functioning member of society.

*There were many opportunities when the defendant might have recon-
sidered the advisability of her actions,* the prosecutor fulminated.

Time, sitting in the tree, peering through binoculars, that I might have had second thoughts. Time, peeing into and emptying out small containers, when I might have pondered, *What in heaven's name am I doing?* and vowed to get on with my life. Time, in the basement, watching the victims' every movement, every intimate moment, through a high-powered telescope, that I might have said, *Enough's enough,* and signed the divorce papers that had been conveyed to me via your attorney. Time, after subduing and tying up the captives (*How to Make Sailors' Knots* figured prominently in the case against me, showing pre-design, devious deliberation, malice aforethought) when I might have looked upon the tableau—my bound and gagged and evidently terrified captives—and reconsidered. Reconciled myself with the past, accepted that you were never coming back; acknowledged that I had crossed the line from unhealthy but legally unobjectionable obsession with my ex-husband and his lover, to criminal offense, punishable in the higher sentencing ranges.

54

FALL 2011

I was not allowed to see or to speak to you. The entry of a restraining order prohibited any and all communications and limited physical contact—assuming, of course, I was able to make the five million dollar bail.

Saul Rubinowitz, Esq., encouraged me to engage an attorney versed in the criminal law. One who would be able to press any and all arguments that could be made in my defense; one who would enable the jury to see me as a human being with frailties, if not a full-blown psychiatric disorder.

"I'm a divorce lawyer," he said. "This is not my bailiwick."

Madge visited me every other Tuesday, chiding herself for failing to recognize the signs of mental breakdown. She cried and said she should have known; she ought to have dragged me to Uptempo more often and encouraged me to mingle. My story of having found love with Todd, the insurance salesman, was too good to be true; she should have recognized that I was not on a tour of Adirondack wineries, as represented, but holed up in a basement, brooding.

"Ophelia, Ophelia." She shook her head. "How did things get this far?"

"I don't know." I hung my head.

"The jury will be able to see how much stress you've been under. That none of it was intentional."

"Maybe." I could only hope that whoever was empaneled to adjudge me would see things from my perspective, but I was not optimistic.

"Can I get you anything? Some reading material? I can speak to your counselor about getting more recreation time. Something to help with the depression."

"Thank you, but no." I rejected her proffer. I told her to leave exhumation of my psyche to the prison psychiatrist. I did not deserve any dispensations.

I had nothing to do but ruminate over the course of our relationship. To ponder how it had all gone wrong, how tender feelings had metastasized into an all-consuming, invasive obsession. How you were willing to throw it all away just to pursue a cunning vixen. How your interest in *getting it on*, in consorting in flagrante delicto at the Minnie Ha-Ha—hours'-long lovemaking sessions, interrupted only by brief, semi-clad forays to the ice box—had destroyed our marriage.

It is difficult to accept that feelings, inevitably, will change. That warm and tender sentiments, no matter how avidly professed, will one day fade into indifference. That a shared life will not continue on, until death do us part, but will be interrupted at some point by a lurid other. That one day the wife will be served with papers seeking dissolution of the marriage in accordance with Article 10 of the Domestic Relations Law. Find herself alone, in a ramshackle Victorian, watching marathons of *Snapped*, convincing herself that she is not at all like the women depicted in the reenactments, any resemblance to living persons or events entirely coincidental.

55

I was mindful of the advice of my criminal defense attorney to sit still with my hands folded on the table. I remained expressionless, particularly when Amber's mother sobbed, screamed *murderer*, and audibly gasped during the more disturbing segments of the coroner's testimony (the judge admonished her to get a hold of herself or she would be forced to exclude her from the courtroom).

I did not visibly react when the coroner testified that in his professional opinion prompt administration of digitalis would have restored Amber's heartbeat; that by withholding the medication I had hastened her demise; that by confining her in a stress position for hours, I had further impeded her circulation; that by stuffing a gag into her mouth (synthetic fibers found in her lungs, Exhibit 27), occasioning respiratory distress, I had, beyond a shadow of a doubt, caused her death.

(My lawyer declined to cross-examine him.)

My lawyer tried, without success, to argue that you were incompetent to testify, that your injuries (the result of blunt force trauma to the head, admittedly inflicted by the defendant) rendered your memory unreliable, your recollections suspect. She tried to argue that your testimony was barred by archaic testimonial privileges pursuant to which one spouse may not be compelled to testify against the other, to no avail.

She elicited an admission that you had, in fact, cheated on me, that you were ashamed of your behavior, that you had chastised yourself endlessly, ceaselessly: what you could have done to avert the fatal incident at the bungalow; how you might have better imparted the news that you no longer loved me, but wished to fornicate with another (you apologized to the jury, but not to me, for your transgressions).

You described how, immediately after setting foot in the

door, I had struck you in the head. Although such a blow is known to produce traumatic amnesia, to impede recollection of events, to make the aftermath of awakening hazy, you were nonetheless able to vividly recount the sensation of awakening, hands behind your back, legs tied to the chair, mouth duct-taped, effectively immobilized (testimony my attorney objected to as inflammatory, prejudicial). You were horrified to discover your betrothed in similar straits, albeit with an improvised gag, rather than duct tape, silencing her.

The jury waited an interminable interval, an unbearable pause, until you were able to go on. You realized, to your horror, that your captor was none other than your ex-wife, with whom you were trying to work out an amicable divorce. You had underestimated (breaking down, sobbing) the extent of the defendant's hostility toward you, reading too much into her surrender of the cappuccino maker, foolishly believing that you could disentangle yourself from the marriage, thinking you were sparing her feelings by neglecting to acknowledge your relationship with the deceased, Miss Amber Halloway.

"If...if only," you stammered, you had taken seriously the defendant's threats to mar your happiness, not brushed Amber aside when she insisted you were being followed by a suspect Volvo; if only you had heeded the neighbors when they reported seeing a figure parked in a vehicle outside your house, late at night, idling in the darkness.

Go on, the prosecutor urged.

You described bargaining for your release. Imploring me to let you go, or at least untie Amber so she could shake off a charley horse or use the bathroom. Perhaps it was unwise, you conceded (stammering, sobbing), to call me *crazy*, to refer to me as a hostage taker, to insinuate that *I wouldn't get away with it*. Perhaps you should have focused on freeing yourself and Amber, rather than revisiting the past, throwing your family's negative feelings toward me *in my face*, describing how they had boycotted our wedding out of a premonition, later proven true, that I was mentally unhinged.

You described how you changed your tack, softening toward me, acknowledging my feelings, admitting you had been a lothario, a faithless philanderer, and begging my forgiveness. *I said whatever I had to say to get out of there*, you sobbed, confirming your lack of sincerity. *I told her what I thought she wanted to hear.*

After a ten-minute recess to assuage your thirst and to gather yourself, we reconvened. My attorney's renewed motion to strike the witness's testimony, *denied*. Her proffer of an expert to discuss how traumatic amnesia impairs recollection of events, *rejected*.

With the jury in thrall, you continued. "She had a hole in her heart," you explained. Perhaps that accounted for her lack of feeling, her deficits in empathy, her refusal to acknowledge, even during the critical stand-off, that she had wrongfully appropriated what was mine, continuing to insist, futilely, that she never knew you were taken, etcetera, etcetera.

You were allowed to testify, over objection, that extreme stress would cause Amber's heart to erupt into an irregular heartbeat. You were allowed to testify, despite vehement protest that you were "not a medical doctor," had no license, and were of dubious competency, that Amber would die if digitalis were not promptly administered.

"Did you warn the defendant of Amber's heart condition?"

"I did," you sobbed.

"And how, if at all, did she react?" the prosecutor prodded.

"She pinched Amber. Said she had good color." The jury elicited a collective gasp, failing to accord me any credit for at least humoring you, for rifling through five suitcases of luggage in search of the elusive heart medication.

"What happened next?"

"Amber lost consciousness. I screamed, but she wouldn't wake up," you stammered. Juror #5 wiped a tear from the corner of her eye.

You looked directly at me, your venom, your contempt, a magnifying glass burning through my soul. I knew, certainly, that you had grown tired of me. You were exasperated by my paranoia, my accusations (later proven true) that you had been up to something. I knew you blamed me, rightfully or not, for the death of Amber, that you held me responsible for the demise of the love of your life, to whom you had proposed that very weekend. I knew you faulted me for my incomplete luggage search, for failing to discover the medication—I tried! I tried!—that might have restored the rhythm of the heart. But I never, *never* thought, before you confronted me in court, before you took the witness stand and pointed the finger dramatically at me—*that's the defendant, sitting there!*—that you loathed me to the quick, wishing I had never existed.

"In your estimation, did the defendant appreciate and understand that the victim suffered from a heart condition?"

OBJECTION. My counselor-at-law jumped to her feet. "He's not competent to testify as to her state of mind, Your Honor. It's sheer speculation. He's not a psychiatrist."

"I'll give him some leeway. I'll allow it."

"Your Honor, with all due respect, he can't testify as to what my client was thinking. He's not an expert on mental states. He's a medical supply salesman. It's highly inflammatory and prejudicial," she continued, exhausting her objections to the proffered testimony. Legally true, but the damage had already been done. The jury had already turned against me. You sobbed, dabbing at your eyes with a tissue the bailiff was so kind to have provided.

"I've made my ruling counselor," the judge asserted. "Answer the question," she directed.

"Yes," you replied. "The defendant knew Amber had a heart condition."

"How can you be sure?" the prosecutor asked.

Juror #10 leaned forward, rapt.

You described how, upon hearing of Amber's putative heart condition, I scoffed and said I didn't care. I was distracted by the surfeit of lingerie in Amber's suitcase, enraged by the discovery of a love note—so much so that I had to excuse myself, rip the note to shreds and stuff it into the garbage disposal—all the while poor Amber lay dying, her heart erupting into a fatal arrhythmia.

OBJECTION, my counselor asserted.

"I've already ruled," the judge sighed.

You described, with excruciating precision, how Amber turned pale, then white, then blue. *I saw the fear in her eyes*, you asserted, purporting to read her mind as well. When Amber slumped over, her heart having failed her, I remained at the table, downing my third glass of gin, deaf to your muffled pleas.

Juror #5 winced. Juror #11 sobbed quietly. Juror #3, who had formed a dim view of me after learning of my role in Lulu's demise, sneered, shook her head, and folded her arms in a hostile posture.

Mallory banged on the door, demanding to be let in. Although restrained, exhausted, and wracked by cramps, you nonetheless managed to hop across the living room and to attract her attention.

Mallory was horrified to discover Amber lying on the floor, tied to a chair, barely breathing. She immediately initiated CPR, while the defendant, i.e., me, stood by, staring into space, detached from the horror of what was transpiring.

Did the defendant attempt to render aid to the victim, Miss Amber Halloway?

Did the defendant snap to her senses, diving in, checking distal pulses, breathing air into the still mouth?

Did the defendant jump on top of Amber, pressing down on the heart muscle, trying to reestablish a heartbeat, to restart the flow of electrical current, one-two-three-four-five?

No, no, no.

After attempting, without success, to reestablish a rhythm, the paramedics declared that *there was nothing further to be done*, disconnected the leads, and discontinued advanced life support protocols. They told you to *look away*, but you failed to heed their advice. You watched, transfixed, as they maneuvered Amber into a body bag, zipped it over her head, and placed her on a gurney, wheeling her over a threshold neither you, nor I, nor the jury—all twelve members—could apprehend.

Ladies and gentlemen of the jury…I, admittedly, engaged in long-term surveillance of the victims. Espied on them from the abandoned and foreclosed-upon next-door property; intruded on private moments; observed them engaged in intimate activities, in private grooming rituals to which no one should be privy, let alone a soon-to-be ex-spouse with difficulties letting go, adjusting to a new reality.

I was not an authorized houseguest; I dropped certain fast-acting soporifics into the neighbor's morning coffee; I pretended to be Crazyforchintz… These are all facts within the voluminous record that I do not dispute.

I do dispute, however, the conclusions to which the prosecutor has attempted to steer you with his heavy-handed theatrics, his eye rolls and exasperated sighs. I am not a monster, a crazed, obsessive ex-wife intent on demolishing my husband's future happiness. I am not an embittered, borderline delusional individual still possessed of the belief (even now, shackled to the counsel table) that he and I can still be together, that we will reunite after the madness of the trial.

What I am, simply put, is a wounded soul. Surely each of you can relate to feeling rejected, to feeling neglected or ignored, even if nothing like maternal abandonment or paternal suicide figures in your past? We are compelled to reenact certain psychodramas, to assume familiar roles, in my case the role of the abandoned, the left-behind one, the one brooding at the kitchen table with a half-eaten sandwich on her plate, and Amber relegated to the thankless role of Bob, used Cadillac salesman, the hapless catalyst, the villain in the Coupe de Ville.

It can be said that I am heartless, that I am cruel, that I exhibited a *callous disregard for life and welfare*. But I wished only to present my side of the story, unexpurgated, without interruption. I wanted them to see through *my* eyes, to feel *my* pain. To see their actions refracted through the prism of my experience. To understand the perspective of the wronged and jilted wife. To understand that sexting is not a harmless diversion, a victimless crime. To admit, once and for all, to fornicating at the Minnie Ha-Ha under the assumed names Mr. and Mrs. Smith. To stealing the cappuccino maker just to spite me. To acknowledge that actions have repercussions. Those engaged in an affair must ultimately be held to account before God, before the courts of justice, before the court-appointed mediator who would divide the marital res, according to the formula set forth in the Domestic Relations Law for apportioning the fruits of the marriage. Etcetera, etcetera.

While they got on with their lives, I was holed up in a basement and subsisting on beef jerky, no one to talk to, no face to gaze upon, no one to touch or to comfort me, my only companion an old shrunken head that had been left hanging from the rafters.

Go ahead. Condemn me. In all likelihood, you already have. In all likelihood, you have disregarded the judge's explicit instructions not to talk among yourselves until after the conclusion of the testimony; in all likelihood, you have been discussing the case over lunch, between breaks, nothing else to do while you are sequestered during trial, banned from reading the tabloids, from watching news accounts of the crime, simulated reenactments on cable networks with titles like *Snapped* and *I Killed my Ex*. In all likelihood, you have already formulated the opinion that I'd gone too far, trailed from too close a distance. I'd eavesdropped on intimate activities, I'd trespassed; I'd kept my husband bound and gagged far longer than was necessary to get my point across, when I could have sent him a vitriolic email instead (I was consigned to self-immolating spam!) or conveyed my displeasure through my divorce attorney like other sparring soon-to-be exes.

But I beg of you to look inside. Tell me, who among you has not been hurt? Who has not experienced the haphazard cruelties of love? Who has not called the estranged object of affection fifty times or more before hanging up? Who has not espied on him from a distance? Trailed him as he left for work? Followed him into the motel motor court, heart aflutter? Who has not conducted an informal background check on his new love interest? Who, among you, has not dreamt of a world in which the new love interest does not exist? Who has not fantasized about the new love interest driving off the side of the highway or smashing into a utility pole (oops, no guard rail)? Who has not wished, fervently desired, for the new love interest simply to be gone, to erase herself from your life, so you no longer have to deal with overwhelming feelings of jealousy and alienation and possible criminal impulses?

So, next time you are gathered around the conference room table, nibbling on a soggy turkey sandwich with a sad leaf of romaine lettuce and globular mayonnaise, engaged in spirited discussion concerning the defendant's state of mind, whether she intended to cause harm to Miss Amber Halloway, or whether it was all simply a tragic accident, whether she understood that Amber's heart arrhythmia, if untreated, might erupt into a fatal fibrillation, or whether she was simply clueless, ignorant as to the workings of the heart muscle, consider this: What would you do if the love of your life walked away, one day, without apology or explanation? What would you do in my place?

56

The jury returned a verdict in under two hours. Not a good sign, according to my counselor-at-law. It was too late, however, to revisit the evidence, to argue more persuasively that I was not to blame, to belatedly accept the prosecutor's plea compromise of ten to fifteen years—earlier scoffed at in my belief, perhaps foolish, that the jury would accept my version of events.

I sat quietly at the defense table as the foreperson read the verdict. As to count one, aggravated harassment in the second degree, what is your verdict?

As to count two, willful and wanton destruction of property (animal rights groups had demanded justice for Lulu), what is your verdict?

As to count three, felony murder, what is your verdict?

I have no memory of the final pronouncement. I blacked out before the verdict was delivered, depriving Amber's family of the opportunity to heckle me, to spit in my face, as I was led in shackles from the courtroom. My exit on a stretcher, with an Ambu-Bag on my face, did not satisfy their need for a dramatic courtroom confrontation, for closure, for an explanation as to why I had confined and subdued Miss Amber Halloway, impeded her egress, failed to heed her pleas, *Please, I'm faint of heart.*

My loss of consciousness did not prevent the entry of a valid conviction or otherwise inhibit the smooth transfer of my person from the county jail to the state penitentiary. Here, I will spend the remainder of my days, serving out my sentence, reflecting on my actions and devising better psychological strategies for dealing with stress and unwanted emotions.

The prison psychiatrist informs me that traumatic amnesia is a common phenomenon. The mind, overcome with stress, flooded with epinephrine, fails to register trauma. The mind, unable to process any more, simply stops functioning.

Stop, it's too much for me.

57

The prison psychiatrist encourages me to confront my mother. To direct my anger and vitriol toward the person who abandoned me, instead of other, less culpable victims. To close my eyes and imagine her sitting on the chair opposite me. To exhume her from the mental crawl space to which I relegated her, long ago. To tell her everything I have kept bottled up inside, everything I have been unable to express, lacking a forwarding address or an intermittent telephone call.

"She's sitting before you now, Ophelia. Tell her what you want to say."

Thus far, I have resisted the good doctor's efforts to engage in one-sided conversation with my mother. To take my aggressions out on a foam pillow, to scream at the top of my lungs.

"You're only eight years old. She left you alone. Wondering where she'd gone to. What do you have to say to her?" The psychiatrist leans forward.

I shake my head. My mouth is dry, my voice gone. The emotions are too deeply buried, in a part of me I've walled off. All the negative feelings associated with her precipitous departure. All the self-questioning and doubts, the unhealthy fixation on Bob's Cadillac Emporium. My inability to make a perfect sandwich, to trim the crusts just so, more evidence of my internal failings, my essential unlovability.

"I can't—" I stammer.

"She's driving down the street. Turning the corner. Bob's arm is around her shoulder. Not even looking back," she persists, painting the tableau.

I resist. I balk at imagining Bob and my mother. The sky-blue Coupe de Ville with the fins. Bob's impatient voice. *What's the hold up?* The clack of the screen door behind her.

"This is the last time you'll ever see her. What do you have to say?"

I do what I could not, lo those many years ago. I leave my half-eaten sandwich. I follow my mother out of the door and into the street. I chase after her, waving my arms frantically. I yell at Bob, *Where are you going with my mother?* I run to her side of the car.

"Tell her what you want to say," the therapist intones. "Look her in the eye."

"Mom?" The sunlight is blinding. All the colors overexposed. "Mom, where are you going?" The aroma of peanut butter on my fingertips. "Where are you going?" I demand to know, though the valise in the trunk and the presence of Bob make the answer self-evident. She is leaving. She is leaving *me.* Our lives diverging, never again to intersect.

"Mom, why are you leaving?" Still, she will not look at me. She looks down, hands folded in her lap. Bob is growing impatient. They need to get on the road by early afternoon or else they'll never make it through.

"Who will make my peanut butter sandwiches? Who will take care of me? Who will love me?" She (the imagined version) does not answer my questions. She remains with her head down, hands in her lap.

"Say what you have to say," the psychiatrist urges.

"Why are you leaving?" I shout, squinting my eyes against the light.

"Why are you leaving *me,*" the psychiatrist prods.

"Why are you leaving *me?*" I scream. The words echoing across the years. Rippling outward from the source of the disturbance. "Why are you leaving me?" The amplitude of grief. The pitch of her leave-taking.

The prison psychiatrist closes the door so my howls do not alarm the other inmates gathered for tai chi in the gymnasium.

58

My hearing before the parole board is tomorrow. I rehearse in front of the mirror. I do my best to appear personable, someone whom citizens would be willing to welcome into the community. I will outline my plans for the future, including volunteer work with women less educated and fortunate than I. I will assure the parole board, through my words and demeanor, that I am not likely to reoffend.

I have not profited in any way from my crimes (though my half-sisters, apparently, have made a bonanza, compensated for appearances in several true crime shows and acting as consultants on *Fatal Obsession*) I live in penury, in ignominy. My academic career for all intents and purposes over.

I will acknowledge my crimes. Take responsibility for my actions. I had no right to snoop, to surveil, to watch you from my perch in the elm. I had no right to invade your privacy, to transcribe your intimate moments, to memorialize what you did on the couch on Tuesday nights. Who among us does not slouch, or skulk, or pick his nose when no one is looking? Who does not eat directly from the jar of sour cream dip? There is no excuse for having intruded on your intimate moments, for magnifying your lives through a short-focus lens. A person has a right to withdraw from view.

I had no right to impersonate a house sitter, or to drug an innocent neighbor, or to look to a Home Depot sales associate for advice regarding cinch ties versus ligatures. I had no right to besmirch your mattress, or your couch, or otherwise to trammel upon your private living spaces. You did not merit my opprobrium, my slurs, my threats to *make you pay*.

Cheating spouse or not, you deserved to be happy. You deserved to be free. You were entitled to your fair share of the marital res. You were entitled to a divorce in accordance with Article 10 of the Domestic Relations Law, having filed and served the papers in accordance with the statute. Adultery is a relatively minor offense, even in Dante's taxonomy of Hell. The adulterous float languidly in the second circle; the murderous and the wrathful rot under a pile of corpses, deep within the Malebolge.

I will urge the parole board to consider my blemish-free record as an inmate. I have not so much as returned one library book late, let alone smuggled in contraband or taken part in prison fights. Any proceeds from the retelling of my story have gone to my estranged siblings and Bob. The so-called "Son of Sam" law requires that I disgorge any profits associated with the recounting of my story. Crime does not pay (literally). A disincentive to those who might commit heinous acts, or go on crime sprees, seeking to immortalize themselves in reproducible media.

It is never too late to find love, according to my fellow inmates. Many of them have admirers on the outside, men whose acquaintance they have made in online forums for the incarcerated and the dispossessed. Men who are unemployed, or on parole, with plenty of time to devote to the epistolary art form.

Perhaps I will take a long overdue trip to Florida to see my half-sisters. The photos—smudged, grainy newspaper stock—indicate that we share a resemblance. A certain similarity in the shape of our faces, in the downturn of the eyes. A far-off gaze, a slight overbite.

My youngest sister is amenable to a relationship, or at least willing to meet me at the Cracker Barrel off Exit 52 on the interstate.

59

O ne day, you and I will be together. Paddling across Lake Mohonk, the sky opening up before us. The valley an echo chamber, *hello, hello*. I will have prepared sandwiches: peanut butter, sliced on the diagonal, with the crusts neatly trimmed. You will gaze lovingly upon me, grasp my hand, wax about the depths of love you feel for me. You will say my name, *Ophelia* (assume, for the moment, that I have been granted early release, that I have been pardoned, that I am somehow no longer under the jurisdiction of the New York State Department of Correction).

Ophelia, may I please have another sandwich? And I will oblige you, taking another from the picnic basket, feeding you, lovingly wiping the peanut butter smudges from the corners of your mouth, probing deep inside you with my tongue, the warm space between cheek and gum ridge, all the crannies and the hidden places.

I love you, I will say.

I love you too, the sky a heartbreaking blue, the blue of cardiac muscle and veinous byways. The sun enveloping us in its warmth. The water deep and impossible to fathom.

I love you, I love you, I love you. The words reverberate across the valley. *I love you, I love you*, the evergreens whispering their approbation. The wind, propelling us in gusts, as we make our way across the water, toward the dock on the other shore.

The paddleboat glides in to shore. I leap up to tie it securely to the piling (the subject of sailors' knots is one we avoid).

The light dappling the water as the day slips away. The night swaddling us, embracing us, as we whisper, *To us*, and raise our picnic basket glasses of wine. The words boomeranging off the rock face, *us, us, us*. We down a bottle of Shiraz, stare up at the stars, at the invisible worlds beyond, the decaying after images of what existed, once, far across the universe. *I love you*, the struck chord of our happiness. The scattered crumbs of peanut butter sandwiches on the dock. The aftertaste of crunchy Jif coats my mouth, making it difficult to speak.

What is love but the union of two souls in search of their lost half? The tourniquet for their bleeding wounds?

Hand in hand, words detonating across the valley, *I love you, I love you, I love you.* I will grip your hand tightly, to ensure that you are still there, not a figment, not the after image of what once was, but flesh and blood, incarnate, real. I will kiss your forehead. I will whisper, *I love you*, the lake glistening below.

Your hand firmly in my grasp.

ACKNOWLEDGMENTS

Thank you to my mentor, Rick Moody, he of unparalleled wisdom; to my early teacher Phil Schultz, who taught me everything I know about voice; to Sheila Kohler and Amy Wallen and the many others who have guided me along the way.

Thank you to Lizz Nagle, my indefatigable champion and cheerleader and exacting reader.

To my boys, one in heaven and one on earth, forever my heart.